The Destiny Doctor

First published in Great Britain 2019 by
Malcolm Spencer

Copyright @2019 Malcolm Spencer

The moral right of Malcolm Spencer to be identified as the author of this work has been asserted in accordance with the Copyright, Designs and Patents Act, 1988.

All rights reserved. No part of this publication may be reproduced or transmitted in any form or by any means, electronic or mechanical, including photocopy, recording, or any information storage and retrieval system, without the permission in writing from the publisher

ISBN 978-0-244-48702-7

This book is a work of fiction. Names, characters, businesses, organisations, places and events are either the product of the author's imagination or used fictitiously. Any resemblance to actual persons, living or dead, events or locales is entirely coincidental.

This book is dedicated to Sir Reginald Watson-Jones (1902-1972) and to his lifetime's work.

Prologue

It's pitch-black, I'm alone. Where am I? Who am I?

I force myself to remember. I cannot see without light, but I can think. I think of light. I feel dizzy, perhaps, I am suffering from vertigo. If I could see, I believe I would be spinning.

The blackness lightens, and I fight hard to combat the nausea. Now, it gets brighter; a sun starts to rise and lights up a landscape. It is not a land I know.

I'm standing on a small knoll with a stick in one hand and a compass in the other. I'm dressed in outdoor clothes and, on looking down, observe that I've good walking boots on my feet; iron-shod with clinkers and triconies, not rubber soles. Why am I dressed like this? And why am I wherever I am? Think.

As the light grows, I can see across an undulating plain, on which there are small clumps of trees and some woods. In the background are hills and further off, mountains, the tops of which are partially covered in clouds. I don't feel hunger and the weather appears to be good. If I want to, I can walk wherever I wish.

Which way shall I go? What's the purpose? A sudden thought strikes me. Am I dead?

It seems logical to walk although I have no reason to do so. It just seems the thing to do. Which way? I choose north with the sun behind me. I start, and, as I stride out memory walks with me.

I take a good look around. From the top of each hill there should be a different view. Maybe, that will help me to find what I am looking for. Which hill should I choose? I choose the biggest one almost straight ahead.

The way at first was very gentle. After a while, I reached the top and could see that the land was even more varied than I thought. It had an infinite variety: slopes, valleys, rivers, and lakes…Straight ahead was yet another hill. It was bigger and looks harder, with a steep slope near to the top, but I feel that, though harder, the reward will be greater. What reward? What am I looking for? Something, or someone, is forcing me to remember memories, as though there is a purpose. I feel apprehensive at being controlled. And with this thought comes some disturbing emotions of fear and guilt. I'm frightened to remember more, but I know that I'm powerless to stop the process. I have to press on.

By this time, I'm climbing up the steep rock face. The apprehension which I had felt earlier has changed to mental and now physical fear; I think I know what is coming next, but I cannot stop the memories.

Chapter 1

1998 December 24th Thursday.

It all began when the chicken shed roof trashed my Volvo.

It was Christmas Eve: there was a gale, a storm, the lights went out and there was a tremendous bang from outside. I went out to see what had happened. There was my Volvo with a chicken shed roof on the top of it. My reaction was to swear and curse, and I must confess at that moment I didn't even consider how the chickens felt.

The day had started normally with the old prostate demanding attention. This is so annoying, particularly, in the Winter when it's still dark and you don't wish to wake up the whole household. You can ignore the reminder, but only for so long. Like a leather log I had rolled out of bed and fumbled round the room, feeling very old.

After the cold totter to the bathroom, the return to the warm snug bed had been, at first, bliss, but then time stood still and there was all the time in the world to think. Initially, in this situation, the mind is totally relaxed; cocooned. You tell yourself that there's time for another hour of sleep, so let it ease back into oblivion. It doesn't happen.

The "inner voice", John McCrone wrote in *The Ape that Spoke*, never stops. The brain logs on and is ready for the *hunt*. One hint and it's racing away like a whippet after the hare; this way and that, into the fields and banks of memory that are waiting to keep you awake.

The monks evolved their marvellous system for organising memory, by imagining their surroundings, their monastery, to be like the present-day files and folders, filling them with facts and storing them in rooms, cupboards, drawers and so on. Thus, a small detail could be located as a knife or fork; or a legal document might be the stitching on a cloak: geography in one room; history in another. You might say memory on a plate! Now I was blaming the monks for this unceasing activity, when all I wanted to do was to get back to sleep.

Don't open the oven door, because the oven contains TAX! INSURANCE! ANNUITIES!

Certainly, don't open the pull-out cupboard, where all the bills are kept, or within a few minutes you will be reaching for the Valium.

This inner voice can also be like water in a sieve, running away so fast, leaving behind just dampness, or, at other times, flooding in so quickly, that it swamps everything, unstoppable, and with a force that tears down mountains or reason. Lie still and try not to listen to the stream as it rushes past.

Christmas Eve, and now about six am. The first waking is normally at five, and the meanderings run for a good hour. Perhaps another half hour before the *Tea Ceremony* starts. This has been somewhat reduced and now means the *Teasmade*. No rustling silk, as an ebony-black-haired oriental beauty approaches with silver salver and tea set, and then gracefully sinks to her knees to serve. Now, there is just the increasing gurgle and spit, which climaxes as the two-minute mangling of the weather forecast comes on. Half an hour more during which to browse the net; not the internet but the intranets of memories and time.

The *plan* was to collect mother from Robin Hood's Bay for Christmas. It sounds a bit like picking up a parcel, and she would indeed have parcels in abundance. Parcels from relatives; parcels from friends in the Lace Society; small dainty parcels wrapped ever so neatly in brown paper and tied with a bow. Parcels slightly torn, with a packet of Maltesers peeping out and a knitted dishcloth on top. A tall thin one - bet it's a calendar (not, of course, of the Ladies of Rylston, that's just come out). Some that rattle; some that smell and some that are leaking making the labels soapy; a box of chocolates: a couple of parcels with no labels so the givers have to be guessed!

From Grisethorpe to Robin Hood's Bay is about two and a half hours, through Ripon, Thirsk, Guisborough, and then Whitby. You *can* go over the moors past Hemsley, a lovely drive in almost any of the seasons, but it takes another half an hour and not to be undertaken if there's fog. Remembering the weather forecast, it didn't sound like fog, which is interesting, because I've no idea what fog sounds like. How does velvet sound, or mashed potatoes?

Suddenly, in my house of neatly housed facts, the laundry door flips open and the shelves inside I can see are stacked with memories of other fogs. Look at them, and they start glowing.

One brighter than the others, that slipped out, brings back the scene on the M62, was it in 1982? Near to Leeds? Huge billows of Dante-like flames; burning lorries, not one but many. The first thing you saw was the glow in the distance, then the writhing flames, red and black, penetrating the grey-white fog, and the smell of burning rubber - you just hoped it was just rubber. Try to let that one, much deeper, fade away but it's too late.

I remembered being seven, going on eight, and walking hand in hand with my Grandmother Walker in a haze that wasn't fog. It was a cloud of dust smoke and steam; early 1941, Liverpool, after the bombing raids on the docks. Coming out of this particular fog, it was still dark, but thank goodness it was time to get up and set off.

The drive over Blubberhouses was pleasant and not shrouded in cloud. This year there was no snow, and the road had been sedated many years ago taking away most of the terrors. Just imagine though, in the past, the track over the moors at night, black, no lights, only rocks, streams and highway men. Little wonder that the country folk thought witches lived up in these hills. These beliefs were slower to disappear in these parts; think of Pendle Hill, just over the border where the last so-called witches in England lived, to be tried and hanged at Lancaster.

Journeys, even in the recent past used to be longer and arduous. In 1955, one journey from Manchester to Saltburn took over eleven hours. To put the length of the journey time into context there was smog - a cocktail of chemicals, laced with sulphur dioxide! The memory is so vivid that even the thought recreates the taste in my mouth and the smell into my nostrils. It was yellow, acidic and tasting of industry; metallic, and sharp as razor blades. It burned the lungs and killed by the dozen every winter. This smog resulted from the incredible amount of smoke which poured into the atmosphere from factories and every household chimney stack. It cannot be compared with the fogs of today. At the time, we thought it was normal.

'Hi Mum! are you ready?'

It was a silly question, because she would have been ready for two hours or more. If you said two o'clock, she would be ready at twelve,

'Just in case you were early,' she said, sitting fully equipped for the worst possible weather. Fur coat, one of three at least, passed on, from sisters and sisters-in-law who had passed away. Hat, also passed-on, packed with tissue paper, to make it fit, with two hat pins to keep it tidy. Hankies stuffed up sleeve. Bright shining leather boots - don't ask where from. I don't think that my mum had actually bought any items to wear for the last twenty years. At nearly ninety, she was allowed these eccentricities.

As a medical register, my mum was almost perfect. She could have filled half of Gray's Anatomy with her ailments; mastectomy, collapsed spine, chronic arthritis, hiatus hernia, and *problems down there*; going blind and losing hearing.

'I'm fine.'

She was a rock, with an immovable faith in her God and her family. I'll bet that mitochondrial Eve took advice from someone like my mum, who would have told her that "daughters are of more use, than sons".

'No, Mum *we cannot take the trolley*'.

The trolley was a ubiquitous metal and plastic workhorse, roughly two feet square, and tool of all trades, which could carry masses of almost anything, to anywhere, as long as the floor was flat. It had two shelves on which, in any normal day, lay pills by the dozen (colour- coded), discarded hearing aids and of course spare batteries, an empty mug, a tea pot, cuttings from the paper, bills and one or two bunches of keys. The lower shelf would at times house the hot water bottle, rugs and the latest lace pricking, or soft toy patterns. The four vertical corners, extending upwards by an inch or two, could be used for handbags (two; one containing the Halifax pass book), the master alarm call button, a surgical collar - I forgot to mention that her neck is playing up a little - scarf and anything which could be hung. Most of the items listed above would be included in the luggage - "just in case" - and all the presents.

'Shall we leave the potted plant? Since it's a Christmas present and you know what it is?' I knew that the Halifax Building Society Pass book would be smuggled in - "you never know somebody might get hold of it!"

'Okay. Let's go, Mum … we've got everything.'

'Don't draw the curtains. Close the doors nearly too. Did you reset the heating?' All of these instructions were delivered in the imperative, with the same authority with which she used to insist … 'and mind you wash behind your ears. Have you got a clean hankie?'

'Yes, Mum'.

The journey back was hilarious, it always was. It's a marvellous foil to have anyone who has true faith and is genuinely good, because the discussions can range far and wide without fear of offence. Any subject, any aspect, will be debated with the same vigour and conviction. When all was said and done the world would be safe for another year.

Chapter 2

Back home with Mum, and the shipment unloaded, it was time for Christmas. The weather had deteriorated seriously and now the wind was howling round the cottage. By the gyrating shadows in the garden, and the shrieks from the nearby trees, any one could tell that tonight was going to be bad. The small shrubs were bent over nearly double and some were broken.

'That *eucalypt* is trying to get back home,' said Sally. Small branches were coming off the trees and knocking on the windows and doors, rat-a-tat-tat, rat-a-tat-tat, then gone to be replaced by others.

'Mum, I think we'll forget about Church tonight,' I suggested. There was little dissension, because it was the Midnight Carol Service in the Garby church, which was poorly attended in the best of times: tonight, I guessed it would be almost empty.

Stoke up the log fire! Settle down for an evening's telly! Listen to the *banshees* outside trying to get in. Plenty of booze, and all the goodies; and stuff the turkey: admire the decorations and the tree.

Our 'tree', was, in reality, an old oak beam, which stands upright as a pillar in the lounge. It was at one time vulnerable to the idea of change - i.e. it was on its way out to the woodpile! The builder, just before applying the chain saw, checked to see whether it was, in any way, connected to the fabric of the building. The answer, as supplied by Penelope in the Odyssey, was still valid and the 'tree', which was in fact holding up the room above, achieved permanency. Both the tree and I are delighted.

At Christmas, the full potential of the 'tree' is fulfilled when it blossoms with cards, which issue from every crack, until it resembles a Picasso-esque painting of a tree, green in Spring then in flames in Autumn; a mass of gold and silver, red and green - all at the same time. Truly a magnificent Christmas tree. I smile when I see the cost of Christmas trees spiralling upwards, faster than the trees can grow: and ours costs *nowt*.

The programme on the television was interrupted dramatically by the lights going out. Batman disappeared with his Bat Mobile and mother woke up. The AGA went into its death throes. For a split second there was silence then, far away, a single dog howled. Mother's comment, 'Oh, no!' matched my expletive and the quite unnecessary explanation.

'Damn! The electricity's gone off. Where are the candles?'

'What about the Tilly?' This from Sally. But we both knew that the Tilly lamp was still broken. Every so often I kept thinking it should be repaired ... that had been several years ago.

'It's broken,' I said in defeat, knowing what would come next.

'I *told* you we should have had it repaired!', replied my darling wife, just to remind me. Yeah yeah, I thought, 'Yes Dear, you are quite right, I should have,' I replied meekly.

Because it was Christmas, there was light; a very romantic light from innumerable candles of all sizes, shapes, colours and smells. This light was, however, not a 'doing light'; it was a light for sitting and dreaming; it was a light to cast moving shadows. It was a light, which had existed before, with plenty of memories, and it started to paint the rooms with overtones.

Where the candles were many and clustered, the light had presence and was hushed as though in church; where singly, or in corners, the candles did not impose, but asked questions from the past. Memories of during the War; listening for the bombs in the cubby hole under the stairs; holidays with Aunts in the country: whispered conversations about girls in scout camp.

There was also the warming orange light and heat from the wood stove, so we wouldn't be cold in *one* room. We could also boil a kettle, fry bacon and eggs on the top of it if the worst came to the worst. I wondered about the turkey.

Most torches worked but gave notice of the intention to quit shortly. I searched for the little camping light operated by a gas cylinder. This still worked.

'I'll put the kettle on while the AGA's still hot. Let's have a cuppa,' said Sally. Within minutes the situation was resolving itself, but I realized that the turkey would have to wait. And *no* television.

'Check with Scottish Power, when they expect it to be back on,' said Sally.

'It's Norweb who are responsible for the supply, *Dear*,' I replied, just to let she-who-knows-everything know that I was on top of it.

The harassed Customer Service Officer had no idea when normality would return,

'Our engineers are working flat out ...' I pictured the team crawling along the road on their bellies, but hastily dismissed the vision. It appeared that the storm had caused a major power failure affecting the whole of the Northwest coast, Cheshire, Lancashire, and Cumbria.

But we're not in Cheshire, Lancashire, or Cumbria,' I protested. 'We're in North Yorkshire.'

'Sir, everything that can be done is being done. I suggest that you try again in an hour.'

Strange ideas started to emerge in the absence of the dark avenger.

'Let's play Scrabble!' Whoopee. Of course, and very soon we would be singing carols, and saying this is how Christmases used to be. Why don't we do it more often? Then, there came an almighty crash from outside and a metallic, scraping, scratching noise. What the hell could that be I thought? There was only one way to find out. With the biggest torch that worked, anorak and wellies, because it was really wet, as well as blowing a gale, I peered out into the storm.

It was pitch black, no village lights, no reassuring glows from the farms; nothing but rain, wind, and things blowing past caught in the cone of the torchlight. My car shone wetly in this light, it still looks black to me I thought, though in the spec it was described as dark blue. But then, I saw that it wasn't its normal shape. Added to its outline appeared to be a large sheet of corrugated iron, rusty and waving. *God dammit! It was a twisted sheet of corrugated iron -* in fact, I realised that it was the roof of Tony's chicken shed opposite!

I reluctantly went outside and, bent double against the elements, clawed my way to the back of the car to see if I could at least get the offending metal off. As I went, I saw the gouges and scrapes along the side, already mentally filling in the insurance claim form:

My car was hit, whilst stationery, by a detached chicken shed roof. No, I did not have my lights on at the time.

I heard another crack then all went black—

Chapter 3

I'm still climbing but it's gone dark again. I've lost the light. I have to pause. In the midst of the absolute darkness a small tendril of thought insinuates itself. I'm Robert Foster, I am Robert Foster ... think. You don't have to stay here. THINK.

1938 April

The name I was given was Robert Foster, but I am normally known as Rob, sometimes Bob or Bobby. I was born in Wincham, a village in Cheshire, three or four miles from Northwich, a town which was built on salt and, because they mined too close to the surface, houses in one part tend to disappear underground every few years.

The locals split Wincham into two, Higher Wincham and Lower Wincham. Higher Wincham, is now where most of the villagers live and where the two schools were located. Lower Wincham was mainly around the canal basin and was known locally as the Boat Road. It was where the barges tied up before going through the Wincham Tunnel, a two mile stretch of canal underground until it emerged near to Saltingsford Locks, and High Leigh. Often you would see the barge horses, or even a couple of donkeys, tied up to the iron rings in the strips of grazing by the canal side or with fodder bags.

Whilst the bargees slept on their boats, they spent their evenings in one of the three ale houses to get their fill before retiring. The *Jolly Jack* was nearly always full in the evenings, whilst the *Rest a While* catered for most of the remainder. The third was further away from the canal, and normally catered more for workers from Brunner Mond, the local soda ash works, now ICI (Imperial Chemical Industries). The nights would be full of singing and laughter with the occasional fight.

Fortunately, the Wincham police station was only two hundred yards away and the local bobby, Police Constable Basin (would you believe that his parents christened him William Charles?) would often as not be in the pub with them. His nicknames were unrepeatable.

Higher Wincham C. of E. School was better known as the Church School, to differentiate it from the Council School towards the other end of the village. All our family went to the Church School, whose classes were about half Higher Winchamers and the other half Boatroaders. The latter had been brought up to be tough but were well behaved, if you didn't cross them.

Of the many games played in the school yard, or on the way home, one was the cause of my first serious accident. "Horse racing" normally comprised two teams of three. Each team had two "horses", invariably boys, who had a rope threaded behind their necks and under their arms, and the reins were held by the "driver" or charioteer, whatever it happened to be called on that particular day. I was one of the horses responding to *Gee up Dobbin* or *Neddy*, or something like that, and running along as fast as we could to beat the other team. I turned my head round as the reins were tugged sideways and hit the sharp edge of the school sign. I went down poleaxed.

They said that I was unconscious for five minutes or so and I was certainly still on the ground when my mother arrived on her bicycle. She had been at Grannie Walker's and had set off to meet me and give me a lift home.

'Can you hold on if I give you a ride back,' she asked?

'I think so,' I said, and managed to stand up rather groggily.

It was only a few minutes to my Granny's where they put me to bed and someone went for Doctor Wilson.

'Concussion is the thing to watch for,' he said examining my bump nearly the size of a duck egg and exactly the right colour.

'Does it hurt?'

'Yes.'

'Just try to sleep,' he said, addressing me, and then my mother,

'If he vomits, or the headache persists, call me back straight away. The bump should go down in a few days and he should be right as rain,' he said. Then, he added, looking at me, 'In the meantime, no school for *you*,'. I smiled.

My head still hurt. Had I slept all night? It was obviously daylight, because the sun was bright, it seemed too bright, blinding in fact. I put my hand up to shield my eyes and encountered a hand, which was hastily withdrawn.

'Oh … he's coming to. He seems to be reacting normally… no sign of him being anisocoric. Splendid.' The disembodied voice went away, and a woman's brown face came close, peering into my eyes; it was a female face, hair in a cap. I struggled to get up. I'd just been clobbered by a school sign, *one way to get knowledge knocked into me*, I thought bizarrely … No … that was years ago. I'm too old for school. This is crazy.

'Easy … easy. Everything's okay. Relax and lie back.' The voice was firm but, at the same time, sympathetic.

'What's happened …Where am I?' The male voice came back this time with a face. It was also a dark face, the face of a man from India or Pakistan. *Has my plane crashed over India,* I thought wildly? This wasn't Doctor Wilson: he was dead!

'How did I get here… and who are you?'

'Hello. I'm Doctor Rashid. You are in the Gardale Hospital. You've had a head injury … but you are okay now. Do as nurse said and lie back.'

'But how——?'

'Lie back old chap. Nurse, a word with you.' They both disappeared out of view. A head injury? I tried putting my hand to my head and encountered bandage, which seemed to run all round my head. Of course. Now, I remember, the car...the storm. The thing on my car. I'll bet I was hit by a flying chicken. But then, rather weirdly, I thought it might have been something bigger, like a sheep... yes, probably, a sheep. The nurse came back into view.

'Do you know your name?'

'Yes.'

'Well, what is it?' She seemed a little impatient.

'Oh. Sorry... it's Bob Foster...er...Robert Foster.'

'And your date of birth?'

'Sixty-four.'

'No, not your age Mr Foster. Your date of birth.'

'Oh, sorry. Nineteen-four... er...thirty-three.

'Thank you. Well Mr Foster, I understand that you were hit by a piece of metal from a building—'

'Was I?' So, it wasn't a chicken or a sheep. 'I'll bet then it was part of Tony's damned chicken shed—'

'Most probably ... Anyway, you had a nasty gash on the right side of your head. We had to operate, but everything's all right now and there seems to be no infection. You will have to be kept under observation for tests until we're sure ... Her voice was getting quieter and I think that I frowned ... she was slowly fading.

I wondered whether it was this bash on the head that was making me feel very strange or was it those two other bumps I'd had when young.

The second was quite simple. I lost my footing on a steep wooded slope when gathering leaf-mould with my Granny Foster and rolled down smack, against a tree. *Wham*. Once again, I was knocked unconscious, but this time only for a minute or two. The bump was in just about the same place but didn't improve on the dent left from the first. Granny Foster rubbed it with goose grease when we got home.

The third was when I failed to negotiate the ninety-degree bend built into the stairs and went slap bang into the wall. The wall came off best.

As I pondered each possibility, the nurse and all around me became slowly more and more transparent, then disappeared. I stopped wondering...

1938 August

It was a beautiful summer day with a light blue sky filled with fluffy white clouds. The corn in the field opposite to our house had just been cut and bundled up into sheaves; four of these were stacked together to form pyramids, or stoops.

The farm labourers had disappeared for the day and it was playtime for us kids. The smell of the cut corn pervaded the whole area, richer than cut grass it smelled golden. Unfortunately for me it also meant hay fever.

I was one of the youngest; there was Billy and Tommy, Iris and Gwendoline, Shirley and Betty. For a while we played hide and seek during which the trick was to get inside the stoop and make yourself invisible, then take your chance and run like mad for the parley tree. If you ran to the far corner you would never make it back before being seen. It was an early exercise in strategy. I had to hide closer because I couldn't run as fast.

Eventually tiring of this simple game someone suggested that we played *Doctors and Nurses*. There was no vote, Billy and Tommy volunteered to take the first turn examining us behind one of the stacks. We had to drop our pants whilst they prodded and laughed. The girls giggled.

Before it was my time to be *Doctor*, I discovered that my hay fever had worsened, due no doubt from hiding inside the stoops, and it was so bad that I had to run home to have my bunged-up eyes and nose bathed. It was always the same, I, being the youngest, always had to fetch the ball or go first through the hole under the wire fence to see if the farmer was in his orchard and, if he did come, I was always the last to get out, being pushed aside by the others. I couldn't wait to be old like Billy.

Nevertheless, I loved harvest time. We used to hang around when the farmers were cutting the corn, although they got angry and would shoo us to the edges of the fields. They would cut from the edges inwards so that, eventually, there would be a small rectangle left. Men would be waiting with shotguns until the panicked rabbits, trapped inside the ever-diminishing uncut haven, would make a dash for it. That, of course, was why we were told to keep well clear.

Bang-bang! Rabbit pie for somebody tonight.

Even as I gazed, the field of stubble lost its golden colour and faded, then it became indistinct as though washed in black ink.

1939 September 3rd Sunday

Friday nights were what we would now call 'party' nights; my uncles Ted and Billy were in their early twenties and had shot guns, which we children were allowed to see, but not touch. Almost every week, if the weather was fair, as dusk was approaching, they would go into the fields to shoot rabbits.

These gatherings were wonderful for me and my cousins. Magically, and mysteriously, it seemed to me, huge pies perhaps two feet across with pastry nearly an inch thick, rising in the middle to a hump, would appear, cooked by Granny Walker. I was certain that each one could feed the whole village.

In the pie there were turnips, potatoes, onions and carrots and, of course, one or two rabbits complete with wonderful rich gravy.

Most men would eat standing up so as not to break up their conversations whereas the ladies would sit at the table. The children would find ledges and try not to spill the food. The feast was washed down by the men with a lot of beer and by the ladies with almost as much tea; the children had lemonade. The gatherings were noisy with chatter, gossip and sometimes seemingly violent arguments – particularly on politics.

Friday night was as ever controlled by my Granny Walker, the matriarch of the family, who ruled absolutely. No-one missed Friday night without a very good reason; it was the gathering of the clan, to communicate the happenings of the week and to sort out any problems which may have arisen. It was also very good for small boys and girls to get up to whatever mischief they could get away with, with some anonymity and protection. In my case, a nearly empty glass of beer was a beacon and a challenge; they never noticed. During the evening I would finish off quite an amount and would go to bed happy.

On this particular Friday night, the men-folk were excited about fighting – but I didn't know who or why; the Aunts on the other hand were quieter, huddled and talking in lower voices.

I don't think that Saturday was anything out of the normal; we played on the swings in the Rec', or Cowboys and Indians in the woods. Sunday, however, brought something very different.

It seemed to me that the whole Walker family had once again congregated at my Grandma's house. As usual, the women were making lunch and the men were drinking pints of beer. I hadn't been told what the special occasion was, but I recognised something was different.

My Grandpa Walker started to fiddle with the wireless. It stood in the living room, on a small table near the window. It was made of some sort of brown shiny wood and shaped like our church window. The front had several black knobs, which clicked when they were turned and above these, what looked like sqiggles in cloth, through which the sound came. It stood silent, until my grandfather switched on the power, which caused it to hum but not talk; then like a magician, he pulled over a switch which looked like a latch on a gate, which suddenly brought it to life with voices or sometimes music.

I was always fascinated by the procedure and had asked him. 'Why do you have to do that, Grandpa?' He explained, pointing to where a wire disappeared through the wall,

'This wire goes up to the top of the house and, normally, you don't want it connected, otherwise lightning can strike down it and burn the house down. But to use the radio I have to connect it. Does that make sense?'

'No.'

He explained about the waves in the air full of music and people talking that he was able to catch when he threw that switch. I didn't understand but it still seemed like magic.

This Sunday, at just before 11 o' clock, all the family gathered round in the room and were unusually quiet, I and the other children were *shushed* and somehow, you knew that this was rather serious. This deep sad voice, said a lot of things, ending with something like "I have to tell you no reply has been received and we are at war with Germany…".

At this my Uncles went mad and rushed into the garden, yelling and thumping each other on the back, which was quite fun, but my Aunts started to cry, which rather frightened me. When we asked why, they said that the men would have to go away to fight.

I wasn't particularly bothered about that but later remembered that this was when things were no longer in the shops. We started to buy tins of food that we didn't need.

It was lighter but I was wallowing in mud, in a marsh, and the stickiness of the mud matched the confusion in my head. Why was I compelled to go on? I

had brought up that innocent memory of the cornfield and then relived it. I was also part of the family gathering. But what was the significance?

Although I did not know it at the time, guns would soon be used to kill millions, people not rabbits, and more than my aunts would be weeping.

I tried to think of some other time.

1939 Christmas Day.

I'd half guessed that there was something fishy about Father Christmas but was told that once you stopped believing he wouldn't visit you. *So*, I believed.

This year there were no new books, they were all old ones recycled. The best was from Uncle Harold, Auntie Lily's husband. It was the 'Bumper Boys Annual', a huge book full of stories and pictures about the British Empire. I devoured it. Canada, with its Red Indians and canoes and huge mountains, enormous fields of corn, huge fish the size of horses. India, with elephants and tigers; Australia with thousands of sheep, and men in cowboy hats and on horseback chasing them. And all these were in the Empire, the British Empire. I was so glad that I was British.

There were also stacks of comics passed on and, of course, there was the party. No matter what was happening in the world it always seemed that Grandma Walker would get everyone together for a party. Only Uncle Joe and Auntie Flo were missing, they had sailed to Australia. Uncle Ted was there with his new girlfriend Grace. She was great fun. Uncle Ted looked exciting in his Royal Airforce uniform.

I was determined there and then I was going to be in the RAF when I grew up. His present to me was a small bible specially made for the soldiers and others in what they called the *Forces*.

Christmas dinner was goose, then pudding with shiny threepenny coins wrapped in tissue paper. The children were always lucky, somehow, and each of us got one. Then it was mince pies and chocolates. The best was a sweet shop into which you put a penny in the slot and then you could pull out a drawer with a small bar of Cadbury's milk chocolate in it. We should have kept those chocolate bars because they were the very last.

1940 April 19th

On my seventh birthday I was given a shiny threepenny bit - to me a fortune. I ran straight to Jones's sweet shop, on the corner at the junction of Stonefield and Lydett Lanes. There were two steps up to the door and a little bell tinkled when you pushed it open. Inside it was cool, and the light had a softness to it, because it came from six small bull's-eye panes in the single window. Mr Jones was a nice old man with a brown smock and little round glasses over which he peered. His smock suited the shop and his glasses mimicked the window panes.

'Now then, what can I do for you, young man?'

'I'd like some sweets please,' I replied, thinking he must be stupid not knowing what he sold in his shop.

'Ah, now then, there is a problem because you see we've run out of sweets. It's the war you know.'

Now I knew that he *was* stupid, because I could see a few small jars of sweets high up on the top shelf. The sweets looked like little gems glistening green and gold.

'What are those then?' I asked, pointing.

'Oh, those are much too dear, those cost sixpence.'

'Well, here you are then, and I pushed two shiny threepenny bits onto the high counter.

'Well, blow me! Where did you get those from?'

'One's a birthday present and the other one is from my Granny's Christmas pudding. I was very lucky.'

'I see. Well there you are then … an' make 'em last, there'll be no more for a long time.'

'Why?'

'It's the war. Sugar's rationed you know; there's not enough to make sweets.'

'My Granny will make some, she can make anything.'

'Not without sugar she can't.'

'She'll make some sugar then,' I replied defiantly. My Granny could do anything.

They were silvery rainbow mints, which reflected colours just like a rainbow when you held them against the light. As I turned one, the colours kept changing red to pink to yellow to blue but then the colours faded as it became sticky. The only thing then was to eat it.

I believe that I hid the bottle because I was certain that divine retribution would fall if it was discovered that I had spent so much in one go. I also felt guilty because I'd eaten them all myself and I knew that that was wrong.

Those sweets were the last which I had for three years – if you don't count homemade wartime ones, from dried milk powder and mint essence. The replacement for sweets after this time became two tablespoons of cocoa in a twist, or a penny-worth of carrots; the former from Jones's, the latter from Burgess's, the greengrocer next door.

For years I had a secret yearning for "Gumboils" which I kept on seeing in the newspapers. There were adverts which showed a boy's face with a large bulge on his cheek, caused, I thought, by an extremely big humbug, or piece of toffee, and it made my mouth water. These same adverts said things like "how to get rid of Gumboils" and I kept on thinking why would they want to do that, I could never get any! When I asked my Grandma Walker how you could get them she said,

'You only get them when you were ill.' Thus, when I had chicken pox, I waited, but the gumboils never came. I didn't complain but thought that you must have to be really ill to qualify!

What I was told, but don't remember, is that we had evacuees from Liverpool in our house, a mother and her two little girls who took over my bedroom. I had to sleep in the box room, which is probably why I have blanked it out of my memory. The good news, as far as I was concerned was that normality returned in the Spring when they scuttled back to Liverpool preferring the risk of bombs to the isolation of Cheshire.

Chapter 4

Think of me. Keep thinking of who you are. Beware of drifting in the past. Who am I?

My name is Robert Foster. I was born on the 19th of April 1933, in Higher Wincham, near to Northwich, Cheshire and lived there until 1951. From 1938 to1944, I went to Higher Wincham Church of England school at the top of Church Road. From 1944, I went to Winsford Grammar School until 1951, when I obtained a place at Manchester Tech taking a degree in Industrial Chemistry. Okay so far.

I received a BSc in 1954 and then had to do two years National Service. I chose the RAF, was selected for aircrew, and did three months OTC (Officer Training Course) in Kirton-in-Lyndsey, Lincolnshire. By choice, I was posted to London, Ontario, Canada (the alternative was RAF Valley, Wales!) and later to Winnipeg, Manitoba. It was at the latter that I met the Walton girls Shirley, aged twenty, the elder, and Sarah who was eighteen. Both were Australian, and both worked in the Royal Bank of Canada, Winnipeg branch. Their father had been accidently killed on their cattle ranch in the outback, near to Cairns, Australia, and the girls emigrated to Winnipeg where they lived with their aunt and uncle.

Shirley was a fantastic dancer and we spent many off-duty hours whirling round dance floors, but it was Sarah who I eventually fell in love with. One thing led to another and Sarah and I spent the weekend before Christmas, 1955, alone, in the log cabin belonging to her uncle, which was situated just outside Winnipeg. No one in the family except for Shirley knew. It was madness, because we both knew that I had to go back to the UK to finish my National Service.

In January 1956 I returned with my squadron to the UK, where I was posted to the Communications Flight at RAF Linton-on Ouse near to York. There I learned how time could be spent, ferrying high ranking officers to conferences - or cocktail parties – and outside "working" hours, playing fives, squash, or roaring round the countryside in high powered cars. I even had a batman who pressed my trousers and polished my shoes.

Sarah - or, as I called her, Sally - and I continued to write to each other and in March 1956 she wrote that she was pregnant and wanted to keep the baby. I was terrified. Sally was only nineteen.

In August 1956, I was able to take a week's leave and flew to Winnipeg to persuade Sally - and her family – that she should come to England with the baby as soon as possible after it was born. After some hectic negotiations, we were married in the Registry Office in downtown Winnipeg by special licence.

The baby was born in September 1956 and named Jaqueline, almost immediately shortened to Jackie. Sally and Jackie flew over in the January of 1957 and we went to live with my mother and father in Saltburn-by-the Sea; they'd moved there in the 1950s. I'd managed to get a job as Technical Officer in the ICI Nylon plant at Wilton.

Jacqueline was christened in February at the Saltburn Methodist church (with some opposition from my staunchly C. of E. family), and in March we had a service blessing our marriage, with her sister, Shirley, as bridesmaid. Everybody came; from all over England, Canada and Australia: it was a riot.

My elder brother, Tom, who was a great electrician, normally worked abroad or offshore, and we rarely saw him, but, when we did, we had some great booze-ups. This was such an occasion. He was best man. His speech lasted until I forcibly pulled him back down into his seat.

From 1956-1968, I worked in the Nylon Plant and Sally got a job in the ICI offices at Wilton Castle, the admin centre for the works. With the help of my Mum and Dad we scraped together a deposit on a small semi' in Marske, which was a few miles from Saltburn. Our second daughter Pamela was born in 1960.

In June 1968, my father died suddenly. Jackie, by then, was nearly twelve and Pam eight. My mother moved to a small cottage at Robin Hood's Bay and I was offered a better job in Lancashire at Yarby Plastics and worked there until April 1998 when I retired. Sally and I found a cottage, named Birchcroft, in a tiny village called Grisethorpe in Gardale near to Skipton, in the North Riding of Yorkshire.

Chapter 5

Wisps of mist appeared... I sensed a warning ...! The scene changed but I retained my identity, it was just like a scene change in a play. I did not go back to that other place. but why was I apprehensive?

1940 June

It was a wonderful summer and my father had arranged to take us to New Brighton for a quick holiday in between a change in his shifts. They used to work three shifts, six-till-two, two-till-ten and ten-till-six, but with the shortage of manpower and the desperate need for what my dad and his colleagues were making, it had been decided to change to two twelve-hour shifts, six in the morning till six at night.

The thought of a holiday away from our little village of Wincham, even though I knew that there would be no bright lights, due to the blackout, made me very excited. I believed there would be dodgem rides and, if we had enough spare coupons, there could be rock; my favourite flavour before the war was aniseed. You could suck on it until all the middle was dissolved then crunch it up in your teeth.
It didn't turn out like that.

There was no rock in the shops and a lot of places were closed. Never mind, there were still donkeys on the beach. These stank of ...donkeys and donkey shit. Holding on to the reins, you were propelled for a hundred yards or so, and then returned, kicking the stirrups madly, which of course made no difference; the donkeys had been there before and seen it all.

Unfortunately, that afternoon the weather changed, and a slight drizzle ruled out an evening on the beach. There were, however, cinemas, and my mum and I loved films so, having looked at the local billboards, we chose to see a Will Hay thriller about *ghosties;* I think it was "Will Hay and the Ghost of St Michael's" ... or was it Old mother Riley? My dad just went along with whatever choice we made.

We were always late. My mother always found that she had to brush her hair or adjust her stockings at the very last minute - she still had some lisle stockings and it was only later that she used to paint a line down her legs - so we had to run along Main Street to the *Odeon*.

Instead of remembering the event I seemed to be there, with my mum and dad at that moment, the actuality clearer than a memory. What is intriguing is that the pictures assumed more shape and texture as though practice is honing the brain to do its job more efficiently, or that I am in some way getting closer to the event.

At that precise moment when my mother stepped off the pavement I saw the shine on the road in front of me. It was still drizzling, and the road was a little slippery. My dad, his hair slicked back with home-made Brylcreem and a slightly craggy face, was laughing, my mother was giggling as she was being pulled along. My little legs had had to go twice as fast to keep up with my parents and my sandals slapped on the tarmac.

As we hit the road with me holding one of my mother's hands and dad the other, her heel went into the slot of a drain cover and stuck. Our momentum carried us forward and we pulled my mother with us. She shrieked and collapsed.

My dad dropped to his knees and lifted up her head, then gently raised her into a sitting position, his arms round her shoulders. She was unconscious but came round slowly.

'Alice. What is it? Are you all right?' he asked. I had let go of her hand and just stood back terrified. What was the matter with my mother, was she dying? Had I done something? To my relief her eyes opened.

'I think I must have twisted my ankle… did I faint? I must have…' said my mother

'Okay, just rest a while. Which one was it?'

'The left one.' My dad looked.

'Yes, it's all puffed up.'

I'd been holding her left hand, so it *was* my fault.

A small crowd had gathered, as they do, asking if they could help. My dad said no, it would be all right. A few minutes later, he asked my mother if she could stand. She said that she could, but clearly couldn't walk far. My dad helped her up, and with her hobbling on one foot, supported by him, we retraced our steps to the digs where we were staying. Now that it was clear that my mother wasn't going to die, I became cross at missing my film, little knowing just how serious an accident it was.

1940 Autumn

It was later that year in the autumn, when it became the season of *scrumpin'* – in reality *stealing* fruit from the orchards, only as kids we never saw that way, it was just *scrumpin'* when we helped ourselves to a few. I went to Aunt Vicky's house because I knew that my uncle had an apple tree, which bore enormous red apples. I went through into the back garden where it was planted. I looked at the tree but saw that it had only three apples on it, and to take one would certainly have been noticed. I thought to ask Aunt Vicky whether one of them was spare. The back door was open, so I went in, but she was out. Then I saw a ten bob note just lying on the sideboard, and, in the same way as stealing apples, just took it.

I knew about money and that it bought things. I'd heard the ice cream van playing it's jungle on Hindley Crescent on my way up Stonefield Lane to my aunt's and ran at full pelt straight up to it and asked for a cornet.'

That's a lot of money for a cornet, young man,' said the ice-cream man.'

'Yes, I know, and I've got to take the change back straight away,' I lied.

The next day with the help of two of my friends, Howard and Bernard, I purchased five Woodbines in their small paper envelope from the newsagent on Lydgett lane, and then, as a reward bought an ice cream for them. It was the cigarettes, which Bernard and I smoked behind the garage of my Granny Walker, that blew it. Howard had run home scared, or with more sense.

The smoke was seen by one of the neighbours as she passed the garage when walking to the shops at the bottom of Stonefield Lane and, thinking the garage was on fire, raised the alarm. My Grandma and my mother, who happened to be at my Grandma's, went to investigate and caught us red-handed and green-gilled. Bernard was taken home to his house, which was immediately opposite, and I was frogmarched home in disgrace.

I realised just how serious it was because there were no leg slaps, which I normally got for being naughty. My dad was on 'nights' and had no inkling until later. My mother told me to put on my Sunday clothes then said,

'We are going to church to pray for you.'

Nothing could have been said that was worse. Church was sacred. It was outside the normal life of school, football, fights. I was a choir boy but that was just attending and singing. I was terrified that my mother was involving God!

We spent an hour praying and discussing it. My mother knelt with me as we prayed and quite often she cried. At the end of it my mother said,

'Now, you must go and apologize to your aunt, and take back what's left of the ten shillings and tell her that you will pay back the difference from your pocket money.'

I did, and worst of all my Aunt Vicky gave me a big hug and said that if I ever wanted a little money to ask for it. Her face was wet with tears. I knew that I would never ever steal again.

The worst, however, was to come when later in the year, my mother's health deteriorated. It was obvious to me that what I had done was causing it. It was punishment. I worked out that the prayers had not wiped out the sin, and my guilt was like a block of lead in my stomach, never to go away.

My mother's problem began with what was thought to be normal backache but, as the weeks went by, the pain grew, and gradually, despite various visits to the doctor and to the Northwich General Infirmary, the local hospital, her health went steadily downwards. She began to double over, which caused internal problems. By the beginning of October she was no longer able to look after me, and I was sent to live with my Granny Walker

'Make sure you take your gas mask with you, said my mother as I was leaving, with my clothes in a suitcase borrowed from Auntie Vicky.'

In 1939, everyone had been issued with gas masks carried in cardboard boxes with your name on the box. There was a loop of string attached to the box so that it could be worn round the neck. The instruction was that they should be carried *at all times*. The signal for a gas attack was that the ARP wardens would go round the streets sounding large rattles.

At school, each gas mask was hung on the back of your desk ready for immediate use but, later on, as the risk lessened, we kept them in the cloakroom.

In our desks we each kept a small tin box containing some biscuits or something similar to eat if we had to go into the Anderson air raid shelter. If there was an air raid, a siren would sound, but we were instructed that we should sit still at our desks until our form mistress blew three blasts on her whistle. This was the signal for us to collect our gas masks and tin boxes and to "walk-not run!" out of the classroom and in single file, climb into the Anderson Shelter, basically a hole in the ground covered with a corrugated iron roof. Fortunately, no bombs dropped near to the school, however each week we practised the procedure until it became routine. It also became an exciting and welcome break from the lessons. No gas was ever dropped, and my aunts started to keep makeup and things in their boxes instead of the gasmasks.

Because Higher Wincham was only ten miles from Warrington and twenty-odd from Liverpool and Birkenhead, the sirens would sound most nights at the end of 1940. Now that I was living with my Grandma and Grandpa Walker, I would often sleep in my Grandma's bed – Grandpa, who worked odd hours at ICI, had his own room. Sometimes it would even be a threesome with my Aunt Lily. Because Grandma was very large, the mattress sagged in the middle and I would keep sliding down the hill to finish jammed to her side.

When the siren went I would be bundled up in a blanket to huddle in the cubbyhole under the stairs until the all-clear sounded. As the weeks went by the raids increased, and my Grandma would try to make us more cheerful by making coffee for us to drink. *Camp Coffee,* which had the picture on the bottle of an Indian Sikh in full dress and turban, was the best. Sometimes we had cocoa instead, plus some home-made currant pie which we called fly-pie.

I was able to visit my mother when my Grandma felt that she was well enough to see me, but I hated it. She was in such pain and doubled up in a bed which had been brought downstairs into the sitting room for convenience. Soon she became unable to get out of it. I had to choke back tears and, later, would cry to myself after seeing her. It was made all the worse because I knew that it was all my fault, both by rushing to see a film and committing a sin by stealing.

In December there was a particularly bad air raid on the Liverpool docks, judging from the length of time before the all-clear sounded. My Grandmother Walker decided to go to make sure that her cousin, Mary, who lived in Smeedon, a small village in Toxteth was safe. The talk on the grapevine was that hundreds had been killed although the authorities were playing it down.

We caught the bus from Wincham to Hartford and then the train to Liverpool Lime Street. When we arrived, we walked in silence past the Victoria memorial, which was still standing amongst the ruins of Derby Square. My grandmother was holding my hand very tightly as we walked through the scenes of utter devastation; houses reduced to rubble; wallpaper flapping in the wind; a girl's precious doll, now in tatters, trapped amongst the bricks which had at one time been a bedroom. Where was the little girl? I wondered but did not ask

I became aware of this strange awful smell, the smell of burnt rubber, wood still burning, mixed in with the sweet odour of roasted meat. I noticed that Grandma had tears in her eyes and was now holding my hand a little too tightly. I remember nothing of the house we visited, nor of Cousin Mary, except for a vague image of a yellow canary in a cage and cats, lots and lots of cats.

It was about then when I started to have nightmares.

Early in 1941, my mother's back got worse, and, as she deteriorated, my father became increasingly desperate. Relatives and friends all had ideas that might help, but didn't, and Doctor Wilson had effectively given up. He advised my father to prepare for the worst.

As a result, my father began to distrust and even hate doctors. One day on returning home, he found a chiropractor in the house trying to manipulate mother's spine. His pushing and pulling was causing so much pain that she was yelling. My dad went berserk and chased him down Stonefield lane with a threat to kill him if he ever came near again. I came to know this by overhearing my aunts whispered conversations.

If it was possible to make matters worse there were many explosions at the Wallerscote plant where my dad worked, and some workers were killed.

I was in fog. I hate fog. In a way it's worse than darkness.

Chapter 6

1953

It was the end of term. Holidays. Therefore, after the traditional all-night game of three card brag, it was time to pack up the washing and a few books and away, for good food, plenty of sleep, and time for body repairs. The transport was cheap. My BSA Bantam, which had a top speed of only thirty miles per hour with a following wind, achieved without any effort at all one hundred miles per gallon.

The *few* books must have bred whilst going into the rucksack and resulted in it becoming so heavy, that, when I finally sat astride my little miniature, it turned over backwards. I finished on my back, still holding the motor bike - upside down, of course - much to the delight of my college chums. With a judicious lightning and re-arranging of the load I set off into the murk.

The visibility was perhaps ten feet., it was therefore with great caution that my bike, rucksack and I wended our way past Hazel Grove into Central Manchester. Unfortunately, when entering Oxford Road, I turned into the wrong lane and discovered the fact only when two red double-deckers hurtled past on either side of me - but going in the *opposite direction*. Appreciating that the odds of their being right was in their favour, and that, even if they were wrong, my Bantam was not a match for a full blooded twelve ton Leyland double decker: I reversed pretty damn quickly.

Once out of Manchester all went well for a couple of hours and I slowly chugged along, at a steady fifteen miles an hour - which, because of the fog, was as fast as most other traffic was going - through Rochdale, Bradford, and finally to Harrogate.

Even though it was still only early afternoon it went quite dark and the fog, whilst no longer yellow, was impenetrable. It also, just to make matters worse, collected on my goggles and condensing in streams, ran down my nose.

Somewhere in Harrogate, I followed, what I thought was a rather narrow bit of road and finished on the top of a four-foot high wall - by one foot wide! It was about this time that I thought that the journey was bloody silly, and this was confirmed, shortly afterwards when I found myself in the middle of a ford. Not a big ford - just a little unexpected.

Standing in the fog, in the middle of a small river, in my full bike gear - second-hand brown phenol formaldehyde bonded glass fibre helmet and black PVC top and bottoms - was a low point. To this day, I don't know where this ford was, having several times tried to retrace my steps to find it. In full daylight, it doesn't exist: there's no such place. It's a ford to Brigadoon. On this night it did, and not being able to see what lay further on, I turned back to Harrogate.

After a cup of coffee from my flask - also carried in my rucksack - I felt better; but still lost. Fortunately, the fog thinned slightly, and some signs became visible. The one which gave me the most hope was the one for Ripon, Thirsk and Stokesley.

Many miles later, the fog had changed to mist and I was able to speed up to nearly twenty miles per hour. Then I recognised a stretch as one that I knew. This was fantastic, and the adrenaline surged through my body. I opened her up a little to a full thirty but, consequently, took the corner a little late. Flying through the air, the hedge, then the barbed wire fence, I thought *Oh Hell! And I still owe for the bike!*"

Chapter 7

Something was interrupting my thoughts. It was a
voice and I tried to ignore it. The voice became insistent.

1999 2nd January

'Hello, hello Mr Foster. Can you hear me?' the nurse's voice penetrated my mental haze.

'Yes … what happened? Am I badly hurt?'

'You've been sleeping, that's all.'

'But I just came off my motorcycle for God's sake … and went through a hedge,' I protested.

'Probably dreaming, Mr Foster; nothing to worry about. You're in hospital. There'll be some food coming soon, and your family are here to see you. Let me just tidy you up a bit.'

It didn't feel like a dream. I could smell the hot oil dripping from the engine as it somersaulted upside down. What was going on?

'Are you all right son?' Mother said, kissing my cheek. Sally was a bit more cautious in case there was still anything from the chicken shed roof on me, and blew me one.

'Yes, Mum, I'm fine; the doctor says just rest, the bruise will go down in a few days you know.'

'What bruise? asked Sally. 'You were nearly decapitated,' She walked away to talk with somebody.

Oh God! I was thinking about that school sign again. It wasn't that was it. It was a motorcycle accident. No, it wasn't that either.

Slowly my thoughts came back to the present. I was in hospital with a head injury. But why all these memories … and they seemed so real. Meanwhile my Mother was talking none-stop.

'I shouldn't talk a lot,' I muttered hopefully.

'…the electric's back on, it's been back on for a week, and the turkey was very nice.'

'The turkey? What turkey?

'The Christmas turkey.'

'… On for a week? How long have I been in here?'

'Eight days. It was New Year's Day yesterday.'

'Happy New Year,' said Sally, returning and blowing me another kiss.

'Happy New Year,' said mother

'Good God! Eight days!'

Now I was panicking. If you spend eight days in hospital, your next appointment was with Joe Preston, the butcher, who was also the Wincham undertaker. He made lovely pork pies but sometimes you wondered where the meat came from… But I wasn't in Wincham, was I? That was then. Now, I was in Yorkshire. I struggled to connect back to reality.

'You were unconscious for most of that time,' said Sally. 'It's great to have you back. How d'you feel?"

'We had turkey pie and chips, it was lovely,' said mother before I had time to answer.

'Turkey pie? Right, Oh, I guess I'm okay.' That turkey pie brought me back with a thump. *Damn and blast*, I thought, that's normally the best meal of Christmas.

'Jackie, Reg and the boys send their love and will come to see you later when you are a bit stronger. Pam has emailed to say you are too old to get involved with garage roofs… but to take care,' said Sally.

'It wasn't a garage roof. It was Tony's chicken shed.'

'It wasn't even a whole chicken shed; it was just part of it,' said Sally. 'You *do* exaggerate. Oh, and the egg man says he's sorry. He's taken his roof back. He said he needs it to stop the foxes climbing in. They found one chicken at Bradfield … on the church roof. The vicar spent days trying to entice it to come down. The egg man told him to shoot the bugger if it didn't. He said he'd even lend him his gun'

'It's Tony.' I said.

'Who, the chicken?' said mum idly, swallowing a grape.

'No Tony's the…. Oh, what's the use.' My head was starting to pound. I closed my eyes and once again saw the smoking Bantam upside down in the field.

'It was my favourite, you know, that Bantam…' I muttered.

'They told me it was a Rhode Island Red, not a Bantam' said Sally but, fortunately, I was nodding off before I went completely bonkers.

Their visit must have been cut short because they'd gone when I was woken up by the arrival of food, which, in my case, was some soup. It wasn't *A la Walker,* which was the soup my Grandma Walker used to make in a huge steaming pot on the gas cooker. The colour varied between a greenish-brown to a brownish-green but always tasted wonderful, a lot better than this, whatever it was: it was also cold.

As I lay there in my paper-thin cotton nightie, I tried to make sense of what had happened to me. The blow to the head, okay. Should I sue? No, I don't think so, but I might be in line for some free-range eggs and I do mean *free,* free range eggs. I slept.

There is nothing quite like the smell and the shiny, glossy, sterility of a sanitised hospital ward. As a visitor, it's not so bad but as a patient … After my nap, I felt better and curious enough tried to raise myself up a little and have a good look round.

God, my head really did hurt, maybe I should ask for painkillers, morphine, cocaine, LSD; maybe a cocktail? *And* I had missed all the Christmas goodies – including turkey pie.

I saw that the ward contained four beds, including mine. Dim huddles indicated that I was not alone. At the moment I didn't care. Moving slightly, it felt as though I had a pumpkin on my head, and I must have made a noise because suddenly there was a rustling noise, and barely heard, rapid footsteps.

'How do you feel tonight?' A different female face, above an enormous bust, loomed into view and I saw that she was another nurse, not the one I had seen earlier, also black, with a kind caring smiling face

'I am okay, just an ache.'

'I will get a painkiller for you. Won't be a tick.' Off she went, and I realised that she didn't click-clack, she squeaked; they must use softer flooring nowadays. Why on earth did I think of tiled floors? Then I dozed fitfully.

At six-thirty the next morning, more or less to the second, there was the clatter of china on a trolley, plus the cheerful chatter of one of the tea lady angels.

'Now then Bert, how are you this morning? Are you feeling better? What would you like?'

'I'd like you to pop into bed, darling.' Bert replied. He occupied the bed opposite

'Oh, you cheeky, young monkey! You're obviously feeling better. Good.' was her riposte.

'Hello Dearie, you Okay? This was to an old Asian patient. 'Here you are, a nice cuppa. Did your children make it last night? Oh, that's good; that was nice for you.'

'Ooh! and who's this? You're new.' she squealed. 'Would you like a cup of tea, Duckie? Milk and sugar?'

I learned later that the tea lady who whisked in and out with the sound of crockery was Beryl. She had a husband, who was unemployed because of a bad back, and six children. I mused that his bad back must be intermittent. After her departure, the ward, which for a few moments had been hyperactive, collapsed back into silence. I sipped my hot sweet drink. It certainly was not *Yorkshire Tea*.

I felt that it was time to make introductions and so, hunching myself up on my pillows, I waved a hand first to Bert who had been identified by Beryl; the man on my far right turned out to be Bill and, finally, to my immediate right, was Abdul, who on a closer examination, was a venerable, old, Indian looking gentleman, now sitting cross-legged on the bed in the other corner. 'I'm Bob', I offered the room.

'It says Robert on your card,' this from Bert.

'Yes, but I'm known as Bob'.

'Are you Scottish? You don't sound Scottish,' said Bert.

Oh! God, I thought this is going to be a bit of a bugger.

'No, I'm from Grisethorpe.'

'What are *you* in for?' asked Bill.

'I really don't know,' I answered truthfully. 'But my head feels awful.'

Quick as a flash, Bert was out of his bed, and was reading the clip board at the bottom of mine.

'Something about you need a lobotomy! No, I'm only kidding. It says *cere-bral con-tusion* or something. I can't make it out. but I think it's your head,' he concluded with authority.

I know that, you idiot I thought.

'You cum in last night. An accident,' said Abdul slowly but precisely.

'Thanks,' I said and wondered if he wasn't a recent immigrant because he had a distinct Bradford accent.

With this, Bert and Bill went into deep discussions about motorbikes and biking. Earwigging, I gather that Bert was an enthusiast who both built motorcycles and raced them. It seemed that he had ridden in the Isle of Man TT.

Bill had been the captain of Bradfield, a local cricket team and had played with several of my friends. It came out later that he had had surgery for bowel cancer and was still on a drip. He certainly wasn't very well and had difficulty in eating even the special food he was given. He broke wind frequently, each time eliciting a loud cheer from Bert.

Abdul was a small, frail figure and quiet; he spent a lot of time sleeping.

We were in Ward 14, Gardale hospital, a sort of general dog's body ward for all sorts - or out of sorts - patients. Bert was recovering from a vein replacement operation and Abdul had a suspected stomach problem and had to have an endoscopy or more correctly gastroscopy, which involved pushing a camera - fortunately smaller these days - down his throat into his stomach.

After breakfast, the doctors did their rounds and mine was obviously a young intern, very new, under training. The crunch came when a rather pretty young woman of about twenty-four, named Sylvia, (as the ID tag on her ample bosom advised) needed to take the obligatory blood sample.

Here we go, I thought, because I knew from experience that my veins were rather cunningly concealed. The first attempt on my left arm was not successful but, nothing daunted, Sylvia tried the right one. You have heard the expression 'sucking air' but this was worse because nothing came out. She then tried to wiggle the needle about, hoping to find something, anything! There was a pause then she said,

'Just have rest for a minute, then I'll try again'. The third attempt was once more on my left arm and, before she started, the increasingly red-faced Sylvia said,

'You don't do weightlifting, do you?'

After several moments, she was sweating, and realised that she had to recover some authority.

'Hmm-mm, we have a specialist nurse who takes the difficult blood samples', she said and whisked away in a flurry of white coat and exasperation. Her exit was not improved when she dropped her stethoscope and tripped over it.

'Damn and blast,' muttered Sylv' hyperventilating.

The nurse, who came some time later, was clearly in charge and would suffer no messing about.

'What's this about the blood sample,' she demanded.

'I think my veins are a bit difficult,' I squeaked, defending my body's reluctance to part with its contents.

'Nonsense!' she threatened and with no more to do went straight in, after a quick wipe with antiseptic.

'Hell's teeth,' she grunted after the second attempt with no more success than with the first. 'It bloody well doesn't want to come out', she growled, giving the impression that my blood was either thixotropic or congealing instantly at the sight of the needle. I can report that the third, or therefore sixth go, was perfect. Thank God for that, I thought.

'You will need a drip putting in later, but the doctor can put that in,' she thundered, and under her breath, 'And the best of bloody luck.'

Time flies when you are enjoying yourself so the two days more that I spent in the bed seemed like two years. On the Friday night before I left, Abdul had visitors, dozens of visitors. They ranged from young men and some very beautiful girls, to families with children of all ages and obviously Community leaders. Abdul held court the entire time sitting cross-legged on his bed but giving the impression of a king with his courtiers. Watching spell bound it seemed to the rest of us as though he transformed from a rather shy and retiring old gent to a patriarch, which, of course, was what he was.

The next day we had the opportunity to chat just by ourselves and he opened up. His English was not perfect but, with prompting, I managed to understand most of it. He was born in Delhi and had fought in the Indian army during the Second World War. Two years ago, he had been invited to Buckingham Palace to receive an OBE "For Services to the Community" and meet the Queen. Furthermore, with a smile, he told me that his son had been selling vegetables on the Skipton market for ten years and had most probably served me.

'What's his name?' I asked. 'I'll introduce myself next time I see him.' Small world, I thought, and wished that communication could have been better.

Just a bit of concussion was the end verdict and I left with some tablets and the instruction to return after a week to have the stitches taken out, plus a warning to take it easy and to ring the hospital if I had headaches or any other problems.

As I left I heard Bert cheer again and hoped that Bill's chemo' would have a successful outcome.

On the way home, in Sally's car - mine had been sent to the garage and was being reconstructed - I wondered about that motorbike journey. I hadn't thought about it for years - nearly fifty years in fact. I survived, as did the bike, apart from a bent footrest. It needed a good clean, I remembered. It, and I, had landed in cowpats! And what about playing in the cornfield opposite to *Broomfield,* our old house on Stonefield Lane. That seemed so real, I had smelt the corn when I hid in the stoop.

I realised that I could smell something now, but it was different, it was a strong smell of coffee? And a German phrase, which I remembered came into my head.

'Ich war dabei.
Ich war dabei.'

1989 9th November.

I was in West Berlin having just breakfasted at the *Best Western* on *Friedrichstrasse*. I was drinking a cup of coffee in the foyer, waiting for our agent to take me to a meeting in East Berlin with Importles, the government agency, which had indicated an interest in buying a patent from us. Suddenly there were shouts and laughing in the street. One of the receptionists was on the telephone. Still holding it, she shouted

'*Blick … auf den Fernseher*! Look at the TV.' We all crowded into the TV room. The newsreader was smiling and repeating:

'*Die Mauer ist offen.*' This I knew was: The wall is open. Wow! The picture switched to a large crowd of people. They were cheering, and people were hugging each other I was flummoxed. What could be happening? The newsreader continued

'*Gehen sie auf die Mauer*'. Go to the wall…

Just at that moment Klaus Niemeyer came in and said,

'Let's go. There will be no work done today.'

We scrambled into his Audi and, as we approached *Checkpoint Charlie*, found it impossible to go any further.

'Let's try walking,' said Klaus and he squeezed the car into an alley.

We walked about a hundred yards but were then blocked by a dense throng of people, there must have been several thousand I estimated.

Then we heard a roar,

'The wall is coming down, and *Check Point Charlie* is open, the guards have gone. Isn't it fantastic.'

A procession of people of all ages surged towards us, and we stood back to let them pass

'They're East Germans,' explained Klaus. He was clearly moved, his eyes filled with tears. Emotions were running so high that even I felt my eyes well up, I didn't quite know why. Everyone was just so happy. People started dancing. We joined in and I could feel myself jigging up and down, up and down. This was more fun than trying to sell a process. I was shouting and shaking hands with complete strangers.

Chapter 8

1999 Jan 6th

'Bob. Wake up ... Cup of tea?'

'Eh. What?' My feeling of ecstasy evaporated as though I had been doused with icy water. I frowned and wanted to get back to that moment. What was it? Was it a dream?

'A cup of tea ... *Do you want* a cup of tea?' the voice was Sally's. She sounded exasperated. 'I've been trying to wake you. You went to sleep as soon as we got you home.'

'And you were snoring,' said mum, looking up from the telly, a repeat of the carol service from King's.

'No thanks... I've just had a cup of coffee.' I answered, and Sally gave my mother a very knowing look and tapped her head.

I was at home, sitting in the lounge in my favourite armchair. So, it'd been a dream then. But such a dream. It felt as though I was actually back on the day when it happened. It was no ordinary dream. Nobody dreams in colour and smells coffee, do they? I thought it must have something to do with my head injury. My memory of that day was crystal sharp, and I remembered my trip to East Berlin some six months prior to the 9th.

I had gone through *Check Point Charlie* with a colleague and with some trepidation, to meet an engineer about a possible deal whereby an East German company would purchase a licence from us to make the new product which we'd developed. Any deal made would be vetted and authorised by *Importles*, of course.

As we entered the DDR, (*Deutsche Demokratische Republik*), we observed that the streets were grey, the blocks of flats made from slab concrete were grey, even the air itself seemed grey. A car was waiting for us and took us a short distance to another dull block of flats close to the checkpoint. We met in a dull office, which was plain and functional with little evidence of happiness and jollity. There was no Pirelli calendar on the wall.

During our discussion I asked the engineer, who spoke almost perfect English, when he had last visited West Berlin. He turned and pointed out of the window to some buildings about four hundred yards away. 'That's West Berlin, but I've never been there. It is not considered wise to allow engineers to visit the West.'

After we had concluded our meeting my colleague and I were driven to a small café close to the railway station to spend our *Ostmarks* (East German Marks) (except for the five *Ostmark* note, which out of cussedness I had hidden in my shoe). The rule was that one was not allowed to take *Ostmarks* to the West - nor to change them into Deutsche Mark.

The *Friedrichstraße* railway station was officially classed as the border between East and West Berlin. It had been built originally in 1870 but significantly modified during the years up to 1939. I read that just before the Second World War, ten thousand Jewish children were brought through this station and then out of Germany to be relocated in Great Britain and saved from the holocaust.

The station had a high vaulted roof and had been quite magnificent with its curved platforms, but now the atmosphere was sinister and authoritarian. *And* it was a dangerous place if you stepped out of line. This was clearly demonstrated on my return rail journey (my colleague had other duties to perform about which I was warned not to ask). Toe the line meant *literally* don't go past the yellow painted line on the platform. It was exactly two metres from the edge, to stop people jumping. The machine-gunners in crow's nests in the roof were there to enforce the rule.

But what a night that had been on the 9th. Everyone wanted to buy us a drink. Quite a hangover the next day, I remember.

I slept a lot during the following week and my head seemed to be healing nicely. At the end of the week, a nurse came to take out the stitches, but I still felt a bit groggy and so was taking it easy. I was concerned about these blackouts when I seemed to go into other places and times; a sort of flashback but not just a memory, much stronger. I seemed to be *there*, actually taking part. Strangely, I felt as though I still had that hangover, but I knew that I hadn't had a drink since Christmas Eve.

Tony came to see me with some more free-range eggs but as he left so did I.

1943

I was reading a book in my bedroom which was about nine feet square and included the airing cupboard. My mind wandered from 'The Pirates of the Air' to the tale about that cupboard inside which, one night, my father cornered a mouse and successfully battered it to death whilst I slept on, oblivious to the noise.

My Aunts refused to believe it, because, when I was younger, they regarded me as the devil incarnate to get to sleep. I was told when I was about two, that my Grandmother Walker was given the job of getting me off and thought to tell me a story. About half an hour later, I crept downstairs to whisper to my aunts that,

'Grandma's sleeping, so we can play some more.'

It must have been about the same time, or perhaps a little earlier, when I stayed with an Uncle John and Auntie Joan overnight. Failing to go to sleep, but obviously tired out, I started to howl inconsolably. After two hours, when they were thinking of infanticide, my uncle told me, I suddenly stopped and announced proudly,

"I can sing a song of sixpence!"

'For *God's sake* then, sing it and go to sleep!' said Uncle John. So, I did.

By three, I was told that I had devised a device of holding open my eyelids. I believed that whilst they were open it would be impossible for sleep to come.

It was pouring down outside, typical in the summer holidays. The 'Pirates of the Air' was becoming a bit boring and I kept remembering the stories my aunts would tell me - some of which I vaguely recalled. For example, at my Grandma and Grandpa Walker's house, *Stonecroft,* I would sit, expectantly, on my grandpa's knee as he, still smoking his hand-rolled cigarette, told me tales from his youth until, as ever, he dozed off. The cigarette would burn down to his moustache, which was originally white but now quite amber through nicotine staining, and the ash would droop almost two inches in a gentle arc before it fell off onto his trousers. At this inevitable conclusion, for which I had patiently waited, I would rush to my Grandma to tell her that,

'He's done it again, Grandma', to see him *walloped* with the rolled-up *Northwich Guardian.* My Grandma was a large imposing lady whilst my Grandpa was small and wiry, so that he always seemed tiny and insignificant beside her.

This morning before the rain, the sun had shone in through the curtains of my bedroom and brightened up the green distempered walls, exaggerating the brush marks and the plaster surfaces. It also lit the ceiling, which was pure white. The woodwork was cream. All the woodwork was cream, but in varying hues, because it depended on which tins of paint had been found and mixed in different proportions. If there was a shortage, paint could be borrowed like a cup of sugar and paid back later, which added to the fun.

Our house *Broomfield* was built in 1936 and was described as a modern-semi. Built to a budget, the fronts were finished in good quality dark, rustic bricks, pointed with white limed mortar, and had bay windows; the back and sides had straight windows with the normal 'commons' bricks. Downstairs there was a small hall with a cubby hole under the stairs; pantry, scullery, living and sitting rooms. Cooking was by way of an electric cooker, with oven, grill and three rings. Heating was by a coal fire in the living room - with a back boiler to heat the water. The sitting room had its own fireplace. There was an electric boiler for washing clothes and a hand mangle.

My room faced the back garden, and, through the simple wooden framed window, I could see the full extent of it and out onto the fields beyond. The land was flat, like most of Cheshire and, at this time of year, was a bright emerald green with growing corn. I could look down onto our garden below, with its vegetables; flowers being a luxury during wartime.

To the left, halfway down the garden was the garden shed looking very old. It was second-hand, unpainted, warped and with its felt covered roof sagging slightly. It was quite a large shed, in fact it had been a small garage. Next to it was our chicken shed housing about half a dozen Rhode Island Reds and the same number of White Leghorns; its run protected by wire netting. Both of these sheds lay at right angles to the concrete path, which dissected the garden and ran the whole way from the small concrete yard to the bottom fence.

At the bottom of the garden on the right-hand side, the inescapable feature was a telegraph pole. It had been installed by the Mid-Cheshire Electricity Supply Company after prolonged negotiations with my father, and its presence contributed a small but regular amount annually to the family income. This pole, bringing electricity into the house, was surrounded by raspberry canes, so dense, that it constituted a tiny forest to a small boy. The remainder of the back garden was filled with cabbages, onions, carrots, broad and runner beans, radishes, and the most important, potatoes; the front lawn and flower beds were occupied not by grass and flowers but by potatoes … and potatoes. The *Grow for Britain* campaign was in full swing.

Anything would grow. To me it seemed quite natural that a packet of seeds shaken onto the surface of the soil, and lightly raked in, would come up as beans, peas, or whatever, two or three weeks later. The secret lay in the soil and the climate. The land in distant times had been a seabed with golden sand, as good as on any beach. Two feet down it lay just waiting to be used. All that this superb sandy loam needed was 'muck' and this was available in plenty from the farms nearby. Even the roads were harvested after the cows and horses had gone by. Out with the bucket and shovel!

Bored to tears I went and stood at my bedroom window. The rain was lashing the back garden and the raspberry canes were bowed in subjugation. *No trips to the woods today, or fishing. Might as well be at school.* I could see further to the right and into the garden of the next door, where lived my Uncle Eddie and Auntie Nellie. They also kept hens, but they had someone special: Billy the dog!

There are personalities which cannot be contained within the confines of one body. Billy was one such. He was a mixed - indeed a mixed up - collie. His coat, black and white in surreal patterns, was always unkempt and normally filthy, but suited to a tee his small head, on which one ear always hung at half-mast. The other ear rotated incessantly to catch the sound of anything to do with food, other dogs, and, in particular, bitches. His nose glistened with health and was permanently in action, confirming the sounds received from the ear and adding its own interpretations about desirability. His eyes, though not as powerful as the other tools, rarely missed much. He rolled them, especially when looking for an escape route, from the hiding, which he correctly thought he deserved and was imminent. If he smelled, it was because he had been through somebody's muckheap, or had been exploring some drain or rabbit hole. He could leap a six-foot gate with ease, anything higher he would climb over.

As a 'rabbiter' there was no equal. When the corn was golden and high, almost ready for harvesting, my uncle would go into the fields with Billy; sometimes I went with them. With sandy banks surrounding many of the fields, there were lots of rabbits. By going to the corner of a field away from their holes, one or two of them could normally be started. Peter would then jump high into the air to see the paths of the rabbits through the corn, and singling out one, would follow it, leaping all the time, until he could pounce. Because of this tremendous talent, there were many rabbit stews to eke out the wartime rations.

Billy, above all else, hated to be confined; this included being chained to his dog kennel. He was strictly an outside dog. His small head was no bigger than his neck; thus no collar could hold him. When he felt so inclined, he would slip his lead and be off. After many instances of thieving, it was decided to appease the neighbours by keeping him inside the shed, but he burrowed underneath it. Then they tried the house; this worked for a while, until he was left alone. The first time he jumped through the upstairs window it was open; the second time it was shut. He dived straight through the glass - and survived!

It was after this that Billy became a legend and any attempt to stop him was abandoned. He lived unfettered for a few years more, but finally got his come-uppance when poison was laid, probably by some farmer who had seen him chasing his cows. If there is a hereafter for dogs, I would like to think of him leaping wildly and ecstatically through the universe, chasing unlimited rabbits, just out of his reach.

The house was one of six dwellings, two bungalows and two semis, situated at the very top of Stonefield Lane, where for the last quarter of a mile, the road dwindled to its original size of a single cart track and was enclosed on each side by a tall hedge.

Halfway along this lane where it kinked to the left, were the 'Three Trees'.

It is worth a little space to elaborate on this lane and these trees. When eight years old, I had twice a week, Mondays and Fridays, to go to choir practice at the village church which was in the old part of the village, at the bottom near to the canal. After choir practice I had to go home along this lane. The only other possible way would have been over the fields.

During the Summer there was no problem and you could saunter along pulling the heads of grass which grew along the banks and perhaps looking at and trying to name the flowers. At the half way point, the three tall elm trees could be investigated. This meant poking about in the large hole in the middle tree, 'the post box', for secret messages, or to check if the 'things' I had hidden days before, were still there, or had been raided. There was no particular hurry, because the later you got home, the later you went to bed. In the winter, it was a different kettle of fish altogether. It was dark, really dark, especially when there was no moon, or there were clouds. Because of the war, there were no street lights anywhere in the village. The houses had no lights showing, only a very faint hint of a glow at the windows with poorly fitting black-out shades. You were allowed to have a torch with layers of tissue paper under the glass front, which did not throw a beam, just a small glimmer, hardly lighting anything, and really so that people could see *you*. My father made luminous materials in his work, these could be made into discs and attached to overcoats, handbags, or the front of bicycles. This again was so that they could be seen. There were lots of accidents. As you approached the end of the road proper and reached Mr Barker's old house, the narrow lane ahead was like going into an unlit tunnel. In the dark this walk was a torture.

My method was, at first, to tread as quietly as possible, so that if there was anyone behind me, I could hear them. Then, to make *sure* that there wasn't anyone, you had to surprise them by suddenly spinning round. You really, *really* hoped that there was no one or nothing there.

The Three Trees was a very bad place in the dark, because you always felt that anyone, or many, could hide out of sight, until you were past, then spring onto you. The tops of these trees grew out over the lane, so that they were on top of you as well. Once past them, breathing slowly, you could walk normally and steadily for a few paces, then run like hell up the lane to the house - hoping to catch them off their guard. At the house there was the front gate – don't even think of shutting it – then the path, round to the back of the house to reconnoitre; but you felt nearer to help if it was needed. When your mother opened the door, you had immediately to revert to the blank nonchalance of a much older person, or perhaps, imitate how one of your comic book heroes, like Chung, the *Wolf of Kabul* in the *Wizard* comic looked, with his cricket bat which he called *Clicky-Ba*,

I think it was about then that I decided, one way or another, that my 'bogey' man had to be faced. It was one early Spring evening, on the way home after choir practice, therefore it was dark. I deliberately made a detour and walked across the fields to the 'Waterworks' Wood.

The three most important woods in my early life ran parallel to Stonefield Lane. The nearest to the village was named Little Bluebell Wood, in the middle, was the Waterworks Wood, and the farthest from the village but closer to our house, was Big Bluebell Wood. Little Bluebell wood was the least interesting, because it was too accessible and open; there was little chance of ever hiding anything in here. It was quite flat and had no ponds or pools. We used it normally for short visits, and, in the spring to see who could pick the longest stemmed bluebell. What the wood certainly did have was bluebells – thousands of them. It was also good for quick games and chases and on one, never to be repeated day, choking ourselves by trying to emulate adults by smoking the pith from the middle of elder branches!

'Big Bluebell' wood was smaller than 'Little Bluebell' wood, why we never knew! Maybe it had been bigger in the past? 'Big Bluebell' wood was the 'full day trip' wood, because it needed time to get there; sometimes even longer, if the farmer was in one of the surrounding fields. Once there, it had pools, with islands and beech trees with rooks' nests, and all sorts of hidden places. It was a magical place and it was there that we chose to have our den.

The Waterworks wood was a cold, mysterious place. The trees were all conifers, so it was very dark and there were no flowers underneath them just a sparse covering of grass. There were a couple of clearings which were full of bracken and brambles. It was in this wood, where I saw my first snake. In the middle of the wood was what had been the waterworks. What was left was a cement foundation and a large underground tank. You could actually see into the tank through a small gap where an iron cover had rusted away. If you got down on your stomach and pressed your eye to the hole, you could see the inside, which was half full of water, and because nothing ever disturbed it, it was crystal clear. It was the nearest thing to a liquid diamond that I had ever seen.

Once, I dropped a small stone into it, to hear a 'plop', which echoed around in the cavern and then saw perfect circles which spread out, silently, hit the sides and return again and again to make patterns. There was another day when we saw a frog, which somehow had got in, swimming perfectly, up and down, up and down, up and down. A few weeks later we saw it's bleached white skeleton lying on the bottom. I remember feeling sad at the futility of its end. Did it realise that it was never going to escape? Did it ponder whether to stop swimming and end it all, or just keep swimming, because it seemed the natural thing to do, until its heart burst?

There was also a gamekeeper, but it was easy to hide from him and only once or twice had we been caught. Even then, there was nothing to steal except pigeons' eggs, so we were just told to clear off. The story was told how my Dad and my Uncle Eddie, got caught by the then game keeper, many years before, in 1936, when they were rabbiting with 'gins' – basically a wire loop tied to a stake. They managed to hide the two rabbits they had caught, before he came up to them, and pretended to be collecting wood. He asked them what they were doing, and my Dad said they were out of work and just collecting firewood. The gamekeeper asked for their names. My Dad said, 'Thomas Black', which was fairly anonymous. My Uncle Eddie was not just as quick thinking and told the gamekeeper, 'Er...er...Earnest Foster'! It took years for my Dad to forgive him and the tale was trotted out at many family get-togethers; fortunately, Eddie's mental block caused no harm as there were lots of men out of work at the time.

This night it was dark, very dark in the wood and I thought that the middle of the small clearing above the water tank would be the best place - because it was the most exposed. I sat down on the ground and waited. I told myself that if anything was ever going to get me it was now. Nothing! So I sat there for about half an hour …. After this I was never ever again frightened by the dark. When I got home my mum said "you've been a long time. Are you all right" and I said, "yes!"

I felt another wrench and giddiness as though I had been on the roundabout at the Rec'. We used to tease the girls when they were eating their chips from the nearby fish and chip shop Then the older girls would grab us and put us on the roundabout and then spin us round as fast as possible to make us feel sick.

Now, it felt worse still, because yet again there was no light. But this time I knew the answer. The only way out of this place of blackness was to wake up.

Chapter 9

1999 Jan 6th

As I got out of the car, I saw that my Volvo was still where it had been when I was clobbered. *I thought that it had gone back to the garage.* As far as I could tell it was the right shape, just gouged a little here and there.

'Have you told the insurance company?' I asked.

'No, I wasn't sure what you wanted to do,' said Sally escorting me towards the house.

'Right.' I knew I felt groggy and confused, but I was sure that I'd done that when I was home before.

'Mother's inside,' she said. 'Probably watching some old movie. The fire's lit so just go and sit down in the lounge.'

'Right.'

'Tony's sent you some eggs.' More eggs I thought; they must be laying well. In the old days the hens used to stop laying in October-November. Had he in fact sent some, previously, or was that just part of the fantasy?

As I walked into the house, it felt as though I was balancing an encyclopaedia on my noggin; if I leaned forward my head would probably fall off. Like the exercise in ladies' deportment, where they had to carry books on their head and walk as gracefully as possible, I tried to imitate them as I progressed through the kitchen into the lounge. The result, I'm afraid, was a complete failure and more of a hokey-cokey than a straight line.

I saw Sally whisper hello to mother, then she put her hand to her lips to tell her not to speak. Mother nodded conspiratorially and returned her gaze to the telly. I noticed that whatever the programme was, it was in black and white. I'll bet the colour's gone kaput and I'll need a new one was my pessimistic thought.

Gratefully I sank into my favourite chair and closed my eyes. I wondered where I would go to next and why?

I was confused. Had I slept or what? I'd just been back to *Broomfield,* our old house in Stonefield lane, in Higher Wincham. By old, I mean where I had lived as a child in Cheshire. That was obviously a delusion. But how could I believe that I had been home from the hospital before? Was that another delusion?

I shouted to Sally in the kitchen. 'Have I been home before now? I mean since my accident?'.

'Shush! I can hear you well enough,' came from my mother. 'You don't have to shout, I've got both hearing aids in.'

Sally came in bearing two cups of tea,

'Not unless you walked home, and then back again to Gardale Hospital; and without anyone seeing you,' was the reply. 'Because I've just picked you up from there. You *sure* you're all right?' she asked standing over me and peering into my eyes.

'I feel a bit confused that's all. I think I heard the nurse tell the doctor something about GCS4, which probably, means gone crazy shoot on sight.'

'Don't be so daft... more likely means there's nothing wrong with you and you're wasting their time. Anyway, drink this tea I've brought you and have a nap.

'Have I had my stitches out?'

'Yes, you had those out yesterday, but you've to see the specialist again at the end of this week. You can ask him what it means' Even though she pulled a smiley face I could see that she was concerned.

'It must be déjà vu,' I muttered.

'Don't know that place…,' said my mother. 'I've been to Belle Vue in Manchester. They'd a lovely zoo there before the war. I believe it's closed now though. Where's that other place? Did you say, *"Daisy-view"*?' That reminds me. Do you remember making daisy-chains at *Stonecroft*, your Granma Walker's house in Wincham?'

'Yes Mum, I do remember making daisy-chains at Stonecroft, but what I said was a French phrase, *déjà vu*, not a place. It means something that seems to have happened before. Because I feel that I've been home before.'

'Well, *of course*, you've been home before, otherwise where would you have slept.'

'You're quite right, Mum …forget it.' Sometimes once she was on the wrong track it took a long time to get her back. And, of course, she was quite right. It did seem a daft thing to say. But in this case, I was sure that I had been back from hospital, twice. The first time must have been a dream, but why was my mind skittering about like this?

My thoughts however carried on from what she'd said. An image came to me, not of Belle Vue, but of the Pleasure Gardens on the South Shore at Blackpool.

Mother and I went regularly for holidays to Blackpool, staying with Auntie Grace's parents, Mr and Mrs Boocock, who kept a B &B hotel in Victoria Crescent, only five minutes' walk from the beach. I also recalled that they had a dog named Nigger who used to chew the legs of the wooden table in the kitchen if he got frustrated.

I would play on the sands, discovering all sorts of things washed up from the sea. One day I found a dead sea-horse. It was so beautiful, but looked improbable, and I couldn't get anyone to believe that such a creature existed. It was another case where there was doubt as to whether it was real, or I had just imagined it. I was justified only years later when Jacques Ives Cousteau presented his films of the undersea world, in colour, and showed sea-horses swimming vertically.

The Pleasure Gardens was a favourite of mine with its *Laughing Policeman*, Dodgems, Big Dipper and many other rides and stalls. One of these was called *the Hall of Mirrors*. In one room you looked down a seemingly endless row of reflections. Was each a world in its own right, not merely multiple visions of the same universe? I felt a bit like that. Was I seeing multiple worlds, or just going plain barmy?

I thought that I'd had the stitches taken out by a nurse the last time I'd been home. Now, Sally told me that they had been taken out yesterday at the hospital. What the hell was happening? Was I simply hallucinating? Were they not dreams at all but alternative worlds? Were my so-called memories true or false? There was also another world out there where I'd been, a very dark world, full of *bad* memories.

It appeared that I was just being taken willy-nilly into the past. Some visions were real, some unreal. I hoped that the first journey home was just another confused vision caused by the injury to my head.

'Nice cup of tea, our Sally,' came from Mother. Then, as an afterthought, 'Who's going to drive me home? I don't think he'll be capable; he's starting to spout about French daisies now.'

I nearly yelled at her *déjà,* ***Déjà!*** not bloody daisies, but stopped myself.

'I'll be driving you home.' came from the kitchen.

'Good.' Mother shouted back, 'Because I think our Robert is a bit accident prone at present. And there are lots of chicken sheds near to Robin Hood's Bay you know.'

If it would have been possible, I would have stuck my fingers into my ears, but that being denied me, I did the next best thing by shutting my eyes and just blanking off this chatter between my mother and the disembodied voice from the kitchen. In so doing, I became aware of a new voice, seemingly nearer and crystal clear. The voice nevertheless was hauntingly familiar. Then I actually *saw* its owner, a young girl of about eight—

'I'm nine' came the retort.

She had mousy brown hair down to her shoulders, dark, dark, gypsy brown eyes, and was walking down a garden path constructed of broken bricks, with a bucket and muttering to herself.

'It's always Vicky and me what 'as to feed t'pigs. Why's it never the boys, Johnny and Bertie?'

She was followed by a girl, I judged to be older, probably by a couple of years, with fair hair and the lightest of blue eyes. Both girls were wearing smocks with a blue-gingham pattern and clogs.

There was something strange about this scene… that wasn't a dream. I wasn't personally in it, I was just an observer. Almost as though someone was telling me the story, their story. I was only 'seeing it' through her eyes. I don't think that this little girl had actually spoken. I was just hearing what she was thinking.

I was thinking that this is really weird, but as yet not unpleasant. Then I realised that something even weirder had happened. The little girl with the brown eyes had answered what I had just thought.

*What's so strange about that. Whoever you are … you're in **my** daydream,'* came the reply. Then, just like a switch being turned off she stopped including me and resumed her conversation with herself.

Them lads can never do anythin' wrong, whereas I'm allus in trouble. Just like the christ'nin' of Billy and Ed'…

The girl following, bumped into the back of Alice and pushed her with her bucket.

'*Her name's Victoria but we call her Vicky.*' She was back in my head.

'Alice, will you stop day dreamin' We'll never get them pigs fed and then we'll be in right trouble,' grumbled the fair-haired girl, who *Alice* had told me was called Vicky. Alice picked up her pace and almost skipped to the pigpen, the irons on her clogs clattering on the path. She opened its gate and both girls spread the swill into the trough in the middle of the muddy floor. Two large pink sows came trotting out to nuzzle lovingly, and noisily, the mixture of potato peelings, scraps of cabbage and other succulent swill items. They grunted their pleasure with their twitching snouts rummaging for the best bits, their disturbingly human-like naked bodies rubbing up against each other.

"*They're called Molly and Polly,*" my narrator told me. The girls, having emptied their buckets, ran back up the path towards the house. Alice was still transmitting. *I want to tell you about that christ'nin'…*

…When we crowded into the church, guess who was pushed up against the radiator? Me of course, and the radiator was red'ot. My leg started to hurt but, when I tried to move away from it, Johnny kept pushin' me back.

"*Ow! Stop it.*," *I hissed.*

"*Shush,*" *said my mother and the Reverend Brindley, the vicar, gave me a solemn look and shook his head. But my leg really was hurting now, and I tried to turn round. This time it was Bertie, who kicked my shin.*

'*Ow!*' *this time I shouted.*

My dad dug me in the ribs.

"*Hush up Alice, or there'll be trouble."*

A minute or too later it was no use; I was burning, so I stamped as hard as I could with my clogs on both the boys' feet.

"*Ow!*" "*Ow!*" *came the chorus. I fled out of the church with my ears ringing from the clip on the head that my mother gave me.*

"*Wait till we get you home, Alice me girl". Her angry threats followed me out into the graveyard. Out of the corner of my eye I saw the vicar shaking his head sorrowfully. I hid behind one of the stones, "Agatha Ermintude Baker 1810-1850 … Sorely missed" and thought I wonder if my mother would* *miss me if I ran away, sorely or otherwise? but I was proper sore and my left leg was red. I spat on it then to soothe it then rubbed it with a dock leaf growing out of a corner of the grave. I was in trouble **again** and it weren't my fault. It weren't fair. So there I've told you. Now go!*

And that was it: end of transmission. This time it was like a radio being slowly turned off; the radio waves might still be in the air, but I could no longer hear them. I was no longer receiving.

1999 Jan 7th

'You look as if you've seen a ghost. Are you all right?' said Sally.

'I don't know,' was my reply. 'I feel very odd.' I was physically shaking. Clearly there was something weird happening in my brain. I believed that I'd just had a conversation with my mother as a girl…but she was sitting watching the telly next to me, not that that mattered if my brain had just made it up.

'Right, we'll ring the doctor.' Sally said peering at me.

'No, just give me a minute … I'll be okay. I've just had a very strange dream that's all. Only I don't think it was a dream. And this time it wasn't me. It was a young girl in a church. Well no, it wasn't actually just a girl—'

'You're not making sense. Was it a girl or not? Surely you know what a girl looks like at your age.'

'I didn't mean that … I think it was *Alice*.'

'Alice? Do you mean your mother? She's asleep.' The proof of the statement came from the loud snores in the chair near the telly.

'I don't know, but I think so.'

'So, it was just a dream, what's odd about that?'

'No, I was in the church and the pig pen with her.'

'The pig-pen! Why the hell were you in a pig-pen? I'll ring for the doctor.'

'No, don't do that, just let me have a word with mother first.'

'I said that she's asleep, so don't you go and wake her.'

'I'll wait.'

'Well if you're sure… but I think I'll go and ring him in any case.'

It was maybe an hour later when the snorting stopped following a particularly loud one. I gingerly got up and walked over to her. One eye opened and regarded me.

'You know you look like the invisible man with his head bandaged up. Only I can see your body, so you're not.' She informed me. I swallowed and ignored it.

'Mother. Did you ever mention a Christening in Wincham Church… when you burnt your leg.?'

'Eh, what did you say? Burnt an egg?... Just a minute while I'll switch my hearing aids on. I always turn them off to go to sleep, you know. It saves the batteries.'

'Please do. No, it was a Christening … when your leg was scalded.'

'Oh, that's better. You mean when Johnny shoved me up against a hot radiator. It wasn't my fault, but I got walloped all the same…it was always—'

'That's it.' I interrupted. 'But did you ever tell me about it?'

'No, I don't think so. I'd forgotten … it was a long time ago you know. It must have been the twins Christening or was it …? I might have done. I'm not sure.' Sally had heard the chatter and now stood in the doorway. It was obvious that she had been listening. She frowned,

'I don't remember you telling *me*,' she said, in an aggrieved tone as though she had missed something, and it was, naturally, my fault.

Mother then proceeded to explain what had happened and how she had been in real trouble when they got home. Only Vicky stood up for her.

I felt the hairs on the back of my neck standing up under my bandage, now that she confirmed that she hadn't told me. I'd been told by a young girl. What was more I had seen and heard *more* than my Mum remembered. I had seen the church and the clothes they were wearing I had smelled the large candle burning near to the font. That German phrase came up again: *Ich war dabei*. But this time I was recalling a memory that I *couldn't* possess; a memory of something that happened before I was born and a vision clearer than my mother's memory.

Sally had indeed rung the doctor and told him that she thought I was hallucinating and was it serious. He told Sally that if I was fit to travel to the hospital to ask for the consultant who had been told about the case.

'Would you feel up to going to see Mr Rashid so that he can have a look at you?' Sally asked me. I said I thought I was.

'Will you be all right Mum. I'm just taking Bob to see a doctor, we won't be so long.'

'Last time I went to the doctor's they kept me waiting for two hours,' Mum replied. 'And what's for tea?'

'We won't be long…and it's fish pie.'

'Not so keen on fish pie,' she muttered then, 'I prefer shin beef and carrots?' Her further grumbles were lost, however, as I was escorted to Sally's car and bundled into the back seat.

Chapter 10

Mr Rashid went through his notes whilst chatting away cheerily, then concluded,

'No, nothing there. It seems the operation went well, with no unexpected incidents. I think that it's just a question of time to allow all the brain functions to return to normal. You had a CT scan when you were first admitted, which showed the trauma and some internal bleeding. The second scan, after the operation, looked normal. If, however, the symptoms which you're experiencing, of hallucinations and confusion continue, I'll recommend an MRI scan, or PET Scan. However, just to make sure, I will book you an appointment with the neurologist, Mr Kassim. Rest assured we will find the answers.

'But what about these hallucinations? What do they mean?'

'Don't worry. They probably relate to something you've heard before but forgotten. I don't think it's anything to worry about. I'll give you some pills to help you sleep. Take a couple at bedtime.'

'Oh, and what's GCS4? I think that I heard a nurse tell someone that I had it.' He laughed,

'You don't have it. 'It's not GCS anything, it's GSC, the Glasgow Scale for patients who are in a coma, and it's just an assessment of how serious the head injury is. There are many other tests, and this is just one of them.'

'Yes, but what does the 'four' mean?'

'By itself not much ... in hospital jargon it means "just a bit confused but open your eyes spontaneously".'

I wanted to ask him what was the worst number; was it one or ten? Then I thought it was probably best to leave it be. Better sometimes not to know.

Back home as I watched with Mother, yet another repeat of *Quo Vadis* on BBC 2, which at least was in "Glorious Technicolour", I mused over that church vision. I knew Wincham Church well because, at the age of seven, I'd been a choir boy. So, I could easily have brought that memory up. Knowing the church wasn't my problem. It was because I seemed to have been present at a Christening many years earlier, and more importantly before I was born. I recalled that in my dream - or what the doctor thought now was an hallucination - everyone was dressed in the correct clothes of the period. If I concentrated, I could still describe each one in almost perfect detail.

A week or so later, Sally was driving Mother back to Robin Hood's Bay, leaving me in the tender care of our neighbour, Liz, for food and cups of tea, Tony knocked at the back door and let himself in.

'I see you're almost back to normal... I just brought you a few eggs...'

'You don't have to, you know.' I tried to seem positive but was actually getting a bit sick of eggs! 'It's very good of you Tony. Sit down, have a cup of tea, Liz has just made a pot...and help yourself to some mince pies. They're the leftovers but they're still good – or Christmas cake if you prefer.'

'Thanks, I will,' he said helping himself to both. 'How d'you feel now?'

'Oh, a lot better. As you can see the swelling's gone down and my head is almost the right shape. I've had the stitches out.'

'Yes, it's more like the coconut it used to be rather than a rugby ball. So, you're not as big-headed as you were!'

'I'll ignore that one. Did you get your chickens back?

'Most of 'em. Some, I think, got caught by foxes. You know there are more here about than you think'

'And what about the one on the church roof? Was it really blown there?"

'Oh, that one at Bradfield. Yes, it must have blown and flown there. The vicar had heard about my shed roof landing on your car, probably from somebody telling the tale in the pub, and reasoned that the hen was most likely mine and brought it back to me in a picnic hamper. I wrung its neck and gave it back to him: it would have stopped laying in any case, you know.'

'Oh,' I wondered what the vicar thought of that, but continued. 'And is the roof mended?'

'Yes, and I've spared no expense and doubled up on the screws. It won't come off again.'

After half an hour of chatting and local gossip, naturally about everyone except ourselves, Tony departed leaving me to sleep and hallucinate about chickens and how they got across the road.

1942

It was two days before Christmas Eve and there was about six inches of fresh snow in the village. My mother and I had been shopping, calling at my Grandma Walker's on the way home. Whilst it was not late, it was of course dark, lit only by the blueish light from the snow. My mother, (for reasons which I did not know until much later in life) was extremely nervous in the dark. She was, if anything, more terrified than me at going up the lane. Holding hands tightly, we walked until just past the Three Trees, when we saw four shadows in the hedgerow. We froze and when they jumped out onto the road, dancing up and down, I am not sure whether it was my mother or I who screamed the loudest.

At this the four lads, who were clearly drunk - probably coming across the fields straight from the Red Lion on Runcorn

Road - realised that they had put the fear of God up us and were immediately contrite, but in coming nearer to apologise, saying, 'Sorry Missus,' only made matters worse.

My mother shouted 'Run!' and we ran and ran, up to the house. As we got close to the front door, however, like a bad dream, something was hanging suspended from it - it was a naked, plucked chicken hanging by its broken neck, legs dangling. This was a very nice gesture by some kind neighbour, but at that time it did not help at all. It was clearly dead and frozen solid, beak wide open and yellow tongue sticking out.

My mother grabbed it and finding her key got us inside quickly through the front door. Heaving and steaming, we stood there, waiting for our hearts to slow, not thinking of taking off our coats, when suddenly there was a noise at the back window.

I had probably read or heard that hairs stand up on the back of your neck when you are frightened, but until then, I had never actually experienced such a thing. The whole of my scalp seemed to be crawling upwards. We listened, and it sounded metallic, like a chain, rattling against the back window frame, then softer noises in the snow-as though something, or someone, was padding around. After a while we thought that it was more likely to be something blowing about rather than, for example, a Nazi parachutist, since no one was actually trying to break down the door.

I'd been told that there was no such thing as ghosts and at this particular moment desperately wanted to believe it. We pulled back the curtain a little but could see nothing outside.

'Open the door and have a look', my mother said after a while, now that we were calmer. Pretending to be brave, I did, but just peered round the slightly opened door into the white haze.

My shriek was echoed by mother, who heard me yell, but didn't know why. A huge, white, shadow, howling, had raised itself up and lunged at me!

'Oh. Billy! Get down! Get down, you daft dog!' For so it was; Billy that monster, who had, this time, not slipped out of his collar, but had actually broken the chain and, just wanting to be with company, had naturally tried to get in. He had even attempted to attract our attention, by standing up at the window- hence the rattling of the links still attached to his collar.

Again, I start to have this feeling of spinning and sickness as though once a game is played, another one starts. This time it's like a panic attack with everything swirling around. There seems this time to be no chance of control; images keep coming and going and all the time a feeling of nausea. Much worse than before, it feels as though my brain is being centrifuged and splattering round the edges of my skull. Now my flesh feels as though it is being stripped away; each molecule parting from its neighbour as if being disassembled and going somewhere else. This has to be stopped, but how? Remember spinning before. When you did your first spin; one minute the horizon stable and very pleasant; the light, clear, luminous, with a view forever and then…

1955 January

The Harvard (mark IV), a 1930's inter-war 100 horse power fighter plane - relegated from active service and now the main weapon in the torture of young trainee pilots, was heading roughly north-west from the Royal Canadian Air Force base at London, Ontario. Inside was Flight Lieutenant Wood, instructor and Pilot Officer Foster; a very green (and soon to be greener), trainee pilot, Squadron 5403. It was a beautiful winter day and the Canadian landscape was white. Lake Ontario sparkled under its frozen, snow covered surface. Without the instructor and allowed to fly just as I wished, the effect would have been magical. But it was not to be.

The initial part of the flight; take–off, wasn't bad, and a few climbing turns, left and right, seemed to please the instructor; thus, it was time to see just how strong my stomach was and whether he could make me sick!

'Climb to 6000feet and level off.'

All the communication via the intercom sounded strange, strangled, tinny and higher-pitched than earthly conversations.

'Yes sir,' wondering what the hell was coming next.

'Keep looking round!'

This yell was accompanied by a sharp kick on the back of my seat. At five feet six and a half an inches I was considered to be within tolerance for a fighter pilot. This was quite practical because, if you were much shorter than this, you couldn't see over the cockpit cowling, which was quite a drawback. Seven feet on the other hand would result in your head being above the canopy.

'Yes sir', I gurgled, wishing for a universal joint in my neck.

'We will now try some aerobatics', he announced in a tone which indicated he would enjoy it, but I might not.

Firstly, *stalls* were a piece of cake.

'Nose up, lose airspeed: stall. Nose down, build up airspeed: level off.'

Stall turns were predictable and fairly reliable.

'Same but when she stalls stick left.' Then we repeated the manoeuvre to the right.

'Good. Now we will do spins,' came the warning.

'Nose up, stall; full left rudder.' The instructor's voice bland.

What had been perfectly controlled and balanced, suddenly became a massive con-trick. The Earth, your friend, which for twenty-two years had been firmly down and the sky immovably up, changed places. The aeroplane was on its back. Then everything was spinning and increasingly faster and faster.

'Stick forward, right rudder until just before it stops spinning, then centralise the stick: slowly level off.' Later he told me that the Canadian Airforce had lost two Harvard Mark II aircraft doing spin training, due to the earlier version having a more stable, flat type of spin, which was difficult to get out of. I was glad that I didn't know that at the time.

How do I, mentally put the stick forward? Close my eyes. Are they open? Think of the horizon spinning but gradually slowing, then think of a rudder reversal. Reverse the maelstrom? Suddenly, the feeling of vertigo and confusion are receding ... going, going ... gone. My head felt like having pins and needles in your arm when you have lain on it.

There's a sense of calm, of peace, but also of weakness, tiredness and a feeling of lack of direction ... At least I felt that I had managed to control my thoughts. Where am I? Where was I? Recap...recap.

I know that I collected mother for Christmas, but I had an accident and since then, like a ship without an engine, I keep drifting, taken purely by the current; where to, where from, seems to be outside my control. That German phrase *ich Weiss nicht wo kom ich her* summed it up. The wrenching feeling appears to come with the changes. Think of way back and no problem. Think of now, just nothing but black. Think of between and it's all hell and confusion!

Have I had a stroke? Is this what it is like? Is part of my brain scrambled and the other perfectly aware, but powerless? Am I trying to reconnect new pathways in my mind? All these questions and no answers! No spinning this time, just a feeling of cold despair.

The hearse drew up outside All Souls with the temporary wartime vicar waiting at the gate.

The church door loomed, and my Grandma was urging me forward to go inside. No, I wasn't going to go in. I wanted to wake up. I didn't want to continue with this dream. The problem was that I couldn't tell if it was just a dream. I was not an observer, it was me. It was my mother who was dead.

Chapter 11

I woke up screaming,

'No … No! Granny, I don't want to go into church.'

'Someone was shaking me,

'Rob, are you all right?'

The room came back into focus and I looked up to see who it was that was asking the question. My heart was thudding. Liz was bending over me.

'Rob I'm sorry I woke you, but you were yelling and shouting. Is it your head?

'I'm okay' I said holding my hands over my eyes. … Just give me a minute.'

'Of course. Was it a nightmare or something?'

'Yes, that's what it was.' I was coming to and my heart was returning to a more normal pace. But I was still scared,

'It was only a bad dream. I'm sorry I startled you. I guess my head does some funny things at times.' I looked round. 'Where's Tony, he was here a few minutes ago?'

'I think he went about an hour ago, he'll be seeing to his chickens. Did you know that he brought you some eggs?' I nodded. 'Liz continued,

'I just popped round to check on you, and heard you shouting. Anyway, you seem much better now, you've got some colour in your cheeks. By the way, what time's Sally due back?

''I think she said about five.'

'Right then, that's in about half an hour. I'll stay with you until she comes.

'Liz, I'm really okay, there's no need to stay ... Really, I mean it. I'm fine ... it was just that bad dream.'

'Right then, I'll just wash these cups up and then be off. What was the dream about?'

'Oh, it was when I was younger, just about seven I think. My mother had had an accident, which damaged her spine and was very ill. I dreamt that my father was killed, then my mother died, and it was her funeral at the Wincham Parish Church.'

'That must have been horrible... *But she's fine?*'

'Yes, I know. It was a sort of a miracle; she happened to be in the right place and was treated by the right surgeon at the right time. My mother was completely cured as you see now.'

'Well then there you are, there's nothing to worry about.'

'No Liz,' I said. 'It was a miracle. But, since my accident, I keep imagining what would have happened *if* that surgeon had *not* been there? And you know, it was a huge piece of luck that he was. Anyway, thanks for coming round, and for the tea. Oh, and Liz, would you mind taking those eggs. I *really* have had too many - just don't let Tony see you.'

'Okay, I'll sneak them out when I leave,' she whispered.

Liz, more correctly Elisabeth, and Len Cooper were our next-door neighbours. Whenever I thought of Liz and Len, I couldn't avoid thinking of the tune from the TV programme Jackie and Pam used to watch ... Bill and Ben, the flower pot men. Sally didn't think it was funny. Liz was a physio at Gardale and gave Pilates classes in the village. Len was an engineer. They were both keen walkers and, whenever they had the chance, jetted off to climb mountains. Len collected Munroes and, I believe, had over a thousand. They were great neighbours and liked to organise events in the village.

After Liz left I started to think about that dream and all the other memories. The episode with Peter the dog has been told and retold, and it still brings tears of laughter, particularly to the youngsters, who love to be frightened. That was an actual happening and most of the memories were of things I had experienced. But some didn't happen. I knew that my mother had been operated on and had been cured. And my father had not died. He had not been killed in an air raid. So, what was the reason for these false memories.

Some were, it seems, dictated to me by my mother, as obviously I could not remember things before I was born. But why were these dreams forced on me? Like the one of my mother having her leg burned in the church; it seemed real, not just a false memory. But where did reality start and stop? If the Mr What's-his-name had not been there to do the operation my mum would have died. What were the odds of that? Particularly during the war, when most resources were focussed on the treatment of wounded servicemen?

It was then that I realised that my right leg was sore. Pulling up my trouser leg I saw that just above my shin was red. Strange. I do not believe that dead people can communicate with the living but if they could what was the purpose. Should I take note? Should I do something? Was I supposed to make sure that what was the present *had* happened or *did* happen! None of it made sense. I'm just rambling due to that head injury.

Over the next month or so, and after several visits to the hospital and specialists, I was considered to have recovered sufficiently to be conditionally discharged, which meant three-month check-ups. Mr Kassim told me that one neurologist, however, had written in his notes that there was evidence of increased activity in my occipital lobe. Apparently, there had been intense research into schizophrenia and other mental problems indicating that reality and imagination flow in different directions in the brain. Visual reality flows from the occipital lobe to the parietal but imaginary visions flow from the parietal to the occipital. So, my brain could be showing my eyes something which was purely in my mind. Okay, I thought, but how did that allow me to hear my mother telling me something that was true, but before I was born?

Although I had been discharged, I was not one hundred percent and spent a lot of time at home brooding. It was a good time I reasoned to do some research. I was intrigued by those flashbacks and, in particular, by the one in which I seemed to be talking, as myself, to that person who just happened to be my mother when young. I have a feeling that psychiatrists and neurologists would be able to write volumes about such people as me but in my low moments felt the titles would be *Nutters and their Dreams.*

I decided to dig out everything I had about my dad and my mother after her accident and how she was cured. Curiously, so far, most of the flashbacks, dreams, or whatever they were, seemed to be centred around my mother.

When my dad died in 1968, I had inherited the contents of his attic which comprised boxes of papers, photos, birth and death certificates, cuttings from newspapers, some books and so on. Those which my mother hadn't wanted were transferred to *Birchcroft.* I brought some of the boxes down into my study to make a start.

The first box was full of photographs and I tried to avoid the trap of looking at them. Once you start you cannot put them down because each one triggers either a memory or a question. We had a number of virgin Ikea storage bins, which were bought *en mass* because "they are so cheap, we might as well get several". I hastily scooped the assortment of black and white, and some sepia tinted photos, into one of them. When I reached the bottom of the box in which they had lain undisturbed for so long I saw that what was left was a polythene wrapped parcel.

'Jeez, that's heavy,' I said out loud. I hefted it and felt that it contained a block or box. I couldn't just put this to one side and I started to unwrap it.

'"Typical dad,' I muttered. It was mummified with Sellotape. There was so much of the stuff, all dark yellow now with age, that I decided to use scissors. A large number of documents, which dad had thought to be important, were ruined because they had been covered in this once clear and pliable sticky-tape, which had degraded into dark brown and brittle strips and which impossible to remove or see through.

Inside was what had been a cigar box, also securely Sellotaped. I used a knife to slit around the lid and opened it.

'Bloody hell!' I cried then quickly looked round. Fortunately, the study door was closed but I knew that Sally had ears like Superman (or, I hasten to add, for the sake of gender equality, Superwoman) and could hear a mouse squeak through three feet of lead.

'Are you all right up there?' Yes, she had heard. I opened the door and yelled back,

Yes, I'm fine… just dropped a book.' I had decided on the instant not to involve her until I had worked out what to do.

'It didn't sound like a book dropping. It sounded like you, swearing.

'I'm fine… no problem.' I thought I wonder if that woman can hear me think; that *would* be trouble!'

It was a gun. In fact, I realised that it was a German World War Two pistol, a *Luger*. What on earth was my dad doing with a Luger? I couldn't resist picking it up. What a beautiful weapon. I released the magazine from the handle; it was empty. Thank God for that. I pulled back the cocking device and, remembering to check that there wasn't a bullet already in the barrel, pulled the trigger. There was a click; it was a click of engineered precision like the car door of a Rolls Royce *Silver Ghost* closing.

Hastily I put it down and, for a while, just sat staring at it.

I looked inside the box to see it there was any note or letter, anything to explain it. Nothing except for a small toy aeroplane in pale greenish polythene and a small square piece of plain polythene with a date on it. I remembered that toy: it glowed in the dark.

Now what should I do? It is not every day that you find a gun, particularly in your dad's things. First, put the gun and the plastic sample back in the cigar box and re-tape it. Then place it back in the cardboard box and pile the photographs on top. After doing this I put the box back in the attic. *Give yourself thinking time.*

That done, I went back to my study and picked up the aeroplane which my dad had made. Just handling it filled me with emotions I hadn't felt for a long time. My eyes filled up. Sally had heard the ladder to the attic being used and yelled up,

'Are you *sure* you're all right?'

"Yes, I'm just looking at some of my Dad's things,'

'Well, be careful on that ladder I don't want any more trips to Gardale. Do you want a coffee?'

'That would be great thanks.'

How well had I known my dad? Not as well as I thought. He had worked at ICI in the Polythene Plant at Wallerscote, Cheshire and then, when the process relocated to Teeside, my dad went with it and moved house to Saltburn.

It was weird that, after my head injury, I had had these flashbacks without wanting them but now, when I was trying to remember things about that period, I found it hazy. I told myself that I was maybe trying too hard. More research was needed. I'd been pretty good at it, after all it had been part of my job. *Okay.* Putting the gun aside, let's find out what we have. And leave the photos just for now. Just thinking about my dad must have stirred other childish memories, or thoughts, and that night I had a nightmare.

It was the end of January 1941. I was seven.

My mother was too ill to look after me, so I was living with my Grandma and Grandpa. The war was going badly, and the air raids were increasing. My

dad and his workmates were working flat out, twelve hour shifts and sometimes doubles.

Things were going wrong at the plant too and there were lots of explosions. One night the works at Winnington was bombed. We all heard the explosions, even under the stairs you could feel the whole house shaking. At last it was over, and we crept back to bed, but I don't think my Grandma slept at all because there were too many noises.

The next morning as I was getting ready for school there was a knock at the front door and she went to answer it. It was a long time before she came back. She had been crying.

'Malcolm, you'll have to be very brave.' My Grandma said and hugged me. I was petrified.

'What's the matter? What've I done Grandma? Have I done something bad? Is it my mother?'

'Love, you've done nothing wrong, it's not your mother, it's is your Dad.'

'What about my dad? He's at work'

'He was on the night shift, but he was killed last night in the bombing.

My world collapsed. My dad was dead and despite what my Grandma said I knew that it was God's punishment. That's why my mum was dying. It wasn't fair they'd done nothing wrong.

'It's not fair, Grandma. It's my fault: I stole that money. My mum and dad didn't do anything wrong. Why?'

It's nothing to do with you love… it's the war.'

The Polythene Plant was totally destroyed, and all production stopped.

I heard people saying that the Luftwaffe had succeeded in destroying most of the Royal Air Force and were preparing to invade. In a seemingly stupid accident Churchill had been visiting a bombed-out part of London and an unexploded mine had gone off. He was dead and the appeasers in the new government started to talk of making a peace treaty with Germany.

Chapter 12

1999

I woke up shouting,

'It didn't happen. You've got it wrong! My dad wasn't killed. It's all lies ... '

'You always get it wrong,' came the sleepy reply from Sally. 'Now go back to sleep.'

It was crazy. The dream seemed so real. It was a dream, wasn't it? Of course it was, but why now? I lay awake in the darkness. My mother was alive. My dad hadn't been killed in a bombing raid, he died much later. Churchill hadn't been blown up. We had won the war not lost it? It was stupid, and I tried to put it out of my mind. All the same I was frightened though by the possibility that it *might have been*. Why did these black dreams keep coming back? Was it the first signs of something wrong mentally, like schizophrenia caused by the accident?

The next morning over a light breakfast I made what I believed was my own spontaneous decision. If I was to understand these odd unsettling flashbacks, I would fill in facts; as it were to put flash on the bones.

'Sally, I'm going to do some work, some research on what my dad used to make ...you know, polythene.'

'Why now?'

'It'll keep my mind occupied and stop me thinking of my accident.'

'Well anything which does that and stops you having nightmares is welcome. Also, why don't you go for a walk? Fetch the paper'

'It's raining … do you want me to get wet in my condition?'

'Hah! Let me know when the baby's due.'

The next day I concentrated on my research. Working might calm me down, bring me back, I hoped, to reality and give my mind something else to think about. And, I had to deal with that revolver.

Polythene (or, as it was originally known, polyethylene) after the war, was marketed under the trademark of *Alkathene*. I still vividly remember my dad handing that aeroplane to me with a smile. It was night-time, he held it up to a light and then switched the light off. It was magic, it glowed in the dark and, as I discovered later, floated in my bath. I now know that it was a model of a two-engine monoplane, like an Anson, or an Expeditor (which I flew in in Canada).

I also remembered that I had written notes for my thesis on polythene whilst at Manchester Tech and still had them somewhere. They were also up in the attic. Sally heard the Slingsby ladder being pulled down.

'Yes, I'm just getting some more stuff,' I called back to Sally. 'Yes, yes, I'm fine! No, I don't want another coffee, thanks.' She was still treating me like an invalid, which I suppose I was. I certainly wasn't going to tell her about my continuing weird dreams.

My notes were in yet another Ikea box - made now from polythene, of course - with some text books all completely out of date. Why didn't I sell them when I could have got a few bob for them? I sold my RAF greatcoat … got £50.

Notes

1. 1898, a German chemist Hans von Pechmann discovered by accident a whitish waxy material, which was in fact a **plastic**. At the time, it was considered to be of no practical use. His colleagues called the white waxy substance **polymethylene**.
2. In the 1930's all the ICI divisions were increasing their research. General Chemicals at Runcorn; Dyestuffs at Blakely Manchester; Fertilisers at Billingham; Explosives at Ardeer and general research at Brunner Mond Alkali division at Winnington. The research director at Winnington, Dr Freeth, increased R&D staff by thirty percent with graduates from universities and also suitable applicants from local secondary schools
3. 1933, two British chemists, Reginald Gibson and Eric Fawcett, in the laboratories at ICI Winnington, under the direction of John Cuthbert Swallow, were investigating the effects of very high pressures and catalysts on olefins like ethylene - a gas - to see whether new organic compounds would result. In one experiment, using ethylene and benzaldehyde in a 50ml autoclave, a white waxy material was found. This was confirmed by Fawcett to be a polymer of ethylene. A further experiment using 1900 atmospheres pressure and a temperature of 170°C gave a better yield. It was discovered that a trace of oxygen in the ethylene had accidentally been present in the pressure vessel and this initiated the reaction. This time there was more interest, but the process was considered to be too dangerous and ICI stopped the research. The research unit was not in any way hidden, but the significance of what it had produced was completely unknown to the general public, and at first, to the Germans. However, Eric Fawcett, who was

disappointed that his research had been stopped stood up at a meeting of the Faraday Society in September 1935 and declared, contrary to the common belief at the time, that ethylene could be polymerised. This disclosure without permission, before ICI were granted a patent for the process in 1936, led to him being dismissed but led to the research being renewed. [Subsequently, all employees were obliged to sign a non-disclosure clause].

4. December 1935, Another ICI chemist team led by Michael Perrin and John Paton, perfected what had been an experiment, with an **accidental** result, into a more practical process. A consultant, a chemist from Oxford university, Paul Hinshelwood suggested the link with oxygen. Over 2% oxygen caused the mixture to explode, 0.002% was optimum. The resident engineer Dermot Manning built stronger reaction vessels out of ductile steel, first 750ml then 2 litres, then 5 litres, and finally a pilot plant was established using a 9-litre reaction vessel, with a blow-down valve which allowed ethylene gas to be pumped in, and polyethylene to be ejected continuously.

5. 1937 IG Farben came to Winnington to discuss with ICI the latest developments and to share polymer technology but failed to come to an agreement. They therefore missed the early development of polythene.

6. News of ICI's patent got to IG Farben and in 1937 their scientists had a copy. By 1938, they also had samples of the product and in 1939 established a small plant at Ludwigshafen. They did not really appreciate the importance of the material, and little polythene was produced until 1944 when the plant was bombed. The equipment was subsequently moved to Glendorf in Upper Bavaria but never produced any material.

7. 1939, production of LDPE (low density polyethylene) began with a 50-litre reaction vessel, producing 100ton per annum capacity at ICI Wallerscote. In 1941, the plant was doubled. Between 1939-1945 a total of 4000 tonnes were produced.

Reading further, I noted that an article said that general distribution was stopped. Why? There seemed to be a bit of a mystery. Ah ha! Of course: the war. The plot thickens. I knew that there was some secrecy about the plant and that there was a connection to WW2 and radar. More digging.

8. Polythene is lighter than water and completely impervious to it and not easily attacked by solvents. These properties were essential in insulating the high frequencies, which were used in the newly developed device, that in June 1941 was called Radio Location Detection and later came to be known as Radar (Radio Detection And Ranging). The development of Radar was described, in the summer of 1941, as one of the best kept secrets of the war having played a vital part in the Battle of Britain (which took place between July and September 1940.

Research was started in 1935, on Radio wave-based detection devices, by Robert Watson –Watt, following a patent granted to him in 1929. He was a leading physicist in the Department of Scientific and Industrial Research, a secret Government committee, headed by Edward Victor Appleton, specifically set up for defence research, in view of the deteriorating European situation. Both of these physicists were subsequently knighted for their work. Sir Winston Churchill, even as early as 1937, was deeply involved in this committee trying to speed up the development because he had correctly deduced the intentions of the Nazis.

There was more, I had forgotten most of it. I certainly didn't know as a boy what polythene was, except a sort of, greyish white, translucent, rubber-like material, which my dad moulded and shaped into all sorts of things from scraps brought home from the plant. He'd been a Dental Mechanic and using moulds made from 'plaster of Paris' - as you would make dentures – he made toy aeroplanes and ships from it. He 'wrapped' handles of knives by melting the polythene, over a flame and then drawing a thread round and round until it was the desired size. Polythene was, without doubt, a new wonder material, which came to be produced in the largest quantity of any plastic. It was, like nylon, one of the original plastics (more correctly thermoplastics). I knew nothing of this but was very happy that the toys he made were almost indestructible. Later my dad went even further and made them luminous like the aeroplane. I had toys that floated in my bath, and which, with the lights off, glowed eerily in the dark. Absolute magic. In my bedroom, I could look at them in absolute wonder whilst going to sleep. Another development was that of threads. My dad showed me that, if you pulled a rod of polythene, it would stretch until it became a thin thread. What I did not know at the time was that it, actually, changed its molecular structure and became stronger. This property was subsequently used to make bulletproof vests.

I did another search, which turned up an interesting comment in a book on international spies and security. In 1935, the German Abwehr got its hands on the fixture list of an ICI plant's football team, which listed where they would play during the season. This included most of ICI's factories and was extremely interesting to Berlin and the Luftwaffe [R. V. Jones Reflections on intelligence 1984.] Fortunately, the polythene plant at ICI Winnington was not mentioned, maybe because it was so small, and consequently was never bombed.]

So, the Germans didn't have the secret of the polythene plant at Wallerscote; they were working in the dark. But why didn't they have this information since they had some of the material? I still felt that my nightmares were in fact just that. But were they? Had in fact something happened?

Why I did not know but something prompted me to take another look at the production sample marked December 21st, 1940. It was a simple square of polythene stamped with the date, time, batch number. Then I noticed it had little dirt marks as though some grit had got onto the surface. I tried to wipe them off with a tissue, but they seemed fixed into the material. Intrigued, I used a magnifying glass to see what they were, but the magnification was too small. I tried with my piece glass (a folding magnifier used to count threads in textiles) with its powerful twenty times magnification.

Wow! There was something in the dots. They weren't just specks of dirt. They were still too indistinguishable to see what they were but there was definitely something there.

Could these possibly be what microdots looked like? I'd only heard them talked about in spy novels and movies. I supposed that to see what was in them properly you needed a microscope or special viewers but as they say there's more than one way to skin a cat.

I had used my SLR (single lens reflex) camera before to enlarge things. The last time had been to photograph and enlarge ticks which Sally had picked up in a walk in the Lake District. The technique was to photograph the object and then to use the Adobe Photoshop programme to sharpen and enlarge the image. In the case of the ticks the technique changed the tiny brown specks, which were about the same size as the microdots, to hideous monsters with a large proboscises and hooked legs.

It worked. Even though the images were very blurred what I saw was quite astonishing. There was a mass of data, letters, numbers, and what I believed to be pressures and temperatures. On one of the other dots there were drawings of what I recognised to be a production line flow plan. I had drawn many such plans of processes so could recognise the type immediately. Logically, bearing in mind the date on the sample and where these microdots were embedded, it must have something to do with the polythene plant my dad worked in at Wallerscote.

 Sally had gone out shopping with a friend, which meant that she would be absent for at least a couple of hours. How they manage to drag out the act of selecting a pound of potatoes and four carrots into two hours defeated me. But, it gave me my chance. I got out the box with the Luger in it and had a good look at it. I was trying to put two and two together. I had a piece of polythene, which seemed to be just a batch sample dated 1940, but had microdots on it, and a gun. That it was a Luger was undeniable. It was the archetypical German pistol which all self-respecting film spies used. I went online, however, and, to my amazement, saw that there were many, many versions. I checked and saw that my Dad's seemed to match a classic p08 or *Parabellum*, whatever that stood for. I looked it up on the internet and discovered that it meant *for war*, which seems appropriate.

 I also took a look at a You-tube video demo of how to strip a Luger, and, after one or two false starts, managed to disassemble and reassemble the gun. I realised what a really fantastic marvel of engineering it was. Each part fitted perfectly. It gave me a thrill just to feel the parts sliding together and clicking into place. It was a strange feeling. No wonder then that there was a market for them. Apparently, they were avidly sought after by collectors, and even fired, in America.

 But, of course, none of this gave me a clue as to why my father had one, or how he had come by it. Had it some significance or was it just something which my dad had picked up in a pub for a few quid? I do remember that many souvenirs were brought back by soldiers after the war. I remember seeing a shell case being used as umbrella stand in somebody's hall, the brass all nicely polished. Gosh! that brought back my memory of the bomb we found in the marshes at Anderton near to the Anderton boat lift. Incredibly, I had forgotten all about that. We three lads rushed the bomb, which was about eighteen inches long with coloured rings round it, to the Wincham police station in a state of great excitement and were told 'to bugger off and drop that thing outside.' It turned out to be a dud incendiary, which the Home Guard or the ARP (Air Raid Precautions) wardens had been practising with and had forgotten.

I ejected the magazine and examined it, remembering that it was empty. I saw that there appeared to be a tiny, tiny almost invisible "z" scratched inside. There was a four-digit number stamped into the top of the gun and some two-digit numbers stamped on various other parts. What did they mean? I presumed that they were manufacturing numbers. To obtain any further information I needed help.

I pondered long and hard how I could possibly progress. I put the magazine back in and hefted the Luger, feeling its power.

Then a strange thing happened I had a clear vision of my Dad smiling at me as though in encouragement. I dropped the gun like the proverbial hot potato. He disappeared.

Chapter 13

I knew that, in my golf club there had been a rumour that one of our members' wife had been at Bletchley Park, something to do with intelligence. I think it came out after a long session at the bar. We didn't talk about it and it was all but forgotten. I knew both Richard and his wife Vera quite well and felt that now was the time to check it out. I needed help.

'Richard, do you think we could have a quiet talk? Somewhere other than in the bar.' I was speaking to my friend in the locker room having just finished a round.

'Sure. Have you got a problem? he asked.

'Just something you might be able to help with.'

'Ok, where do you have in mind?'

'The Devonshire.'

'What now? I was just fancying a pint.'

'Unless it's inconvenient. I'm buying. You can have the pint at the Devonshire, and I owe you for the game.'

'Well then, okay… *and lunch*. Remember we agreed lunch as well? What's the mystery…you're a bit old for a paternity suit?'

Richard and I had been friends for many years. He was well over six feet although now with a slight stoop. He had blue eyes and had had a shock of blond hair when I first knew him, now most of it had disappeared with the years. In his younger days he'd been a good tennis player, playing for Yorkshire and still played occasionally at the local tennis club, even though he'd turned eighty. His golf handicap was eighteen but in his younger years he had been a single figure man and he was difficult to beat even with him giving extra shots. He had been a solicitor for many years in the local firm of solicitors, when it was Hayes, Bowden, and Yardley, he'd been the Bowden bit.

I thought the simplest thing was to tell him that I had found something *odd* in my dad's belongings. I explained that it was only after my accident that I had started to investigate the boxes which had been stored in the attic. Then I could gradually introduce the possibility of discussing it with his wife.

'Oh, you mean after you'd flown the coop…or rather it had flown at you.' He chuckled.

'Yeah yeah…ha-ha… I know it was a scream, I'm only just living it down. The other one is 'you nearly got a birdie'. No, it's nothing to do with that…or only slightly'

'Well, cough it up. What then.'

'To put it bluntly, I found a gun, which, I'm certain, is a German Luger … in my dad's belongings.'

All the banter disappeared as he absorbed the news, his demeanour became professional.

'Ah. That does paint a different picture. I don't suppose you've contacted the police?'

'No, I haven't.'

'I see. Do you have any idea where he might have got it from? I don't suppose you know if he had a gun licence?'

No and no; no idea, and as far as I know, no licence. I certainly haven't found one'

'Anything else to go on?'

'I think it's a Luger Mauser p08, I looked it up on the internet. I believe another name is Parabellum. I looked that up as well'

'Ah. "*Si vis pacem, para bellum*" if you want peace prepare for war. You've done your homework it appears. Well, then, what do you think I can do?'

'Actually… to be truthful, it wasn't you I was thinking of…'

'Oh. How d'you mean? If it's not me why ask me…Hmm …Ah?' There was a longish pause then as the penny dropped, 'I'm beginning to understand now. You want me to have a word with Vera?'

'Yes, I did mean Vera,' I admitted '… but I thought to ask you first.' He picked up his pint and swirled the foamy *Black Sheep* round and round, then put it carefully back on the table, and looked at me straight in the eye … hard.

'Why do you think that Vera might be able to help?'

'I am not sure if she can, but …you know…' I hesitated, wanting him to help me out.

'I see.' There was another long pause during which he continued to stare at me. 'How did you know?'

'Sorry to mention it… there's been a rumour for some years, you know – or maybe you didn't? Look, I'm grasping at straws. I've got a pistol, which could have been bought in a pub after the war, *or*, I wonder if there could be any possible connection to the fact that my dad worked in the production of the plastic material, polythene, which was quite hush-hush during the war because it was used in Radar equipment.' All of this came out in a rush. I took a breath and continued.

'He was a foreman in the Polythene Plant at Wallerscote, part of the ICI complex at Winnington, Cheshire. I discovered recently that the Germans before the war in 1939, had the locations of all the ICI factories *except* for the Polythene Plant. I remember my dad putting his finger to his lips and telling me, after the war, that it had been very hush-hush. But this could all be fantasy and it's true that I've been having strange dreams since my accident. Perhaps it would be better to forget it?'

'Well, it does seem to be a bit far-fetched to start with, and I cannot, myself, see why you've connected the two. The pub route surely is the most obvious one. You know that I was a major in the Cheshires, and there were many times when I thought of holding onto my Enfield revolver when I was demobbed. But I resisted the temptation. I must confess that, whilst I was still in harness, I wished that I'd kept that revolver to use on one or two of my more difficult clients.'

'I know what you mean. I had a customer who kept a colt pistol on the wall by his desk. When I enquired about the bill he owed he slowly took it down and pointed it at me. Just for a second I did wonder if it was loaded.'

Hmm... I've never had that. Anyway... back to your problem. I really don't think that Vera can be of help, but I'll mention it to her. If she wishes to get involved that's up to her, I've no objections. Is there anything else to go on?'

'Not much but I'm still looking. And thanks, I appreciate it. Oh, to put your mind at rest there are no bullets, just the gun.'

I didn't mention that I also had a chip of polythene with what looked like microdots in it. That might have seemed just too implausible for words and destroy any credibility I might have had.

'You know,' said Richard drily. 'I feel rather peckish now, and I rather like the idea of that roast pheasant. And, perhaps, a nice bottle of St Émilion to wash it down. What do you think?'

Back home, feeling fuller and definitely mellower after the lunch which had been larger than the sandwiches I had planned, Sally tut-tutted and shook her head,

'Drunk midweek ...it won't do your head any good you know. And don't think I'll be traipsing up and down these stairs to bring you coffee ...' Retiring to the more peaceful haven of my study, I unearthed several books about the ICI group to try to piece together what the process had been like in the 1940's.

We were of course never allowed near the place, but we could look across the river at it. My dad had told me, when I about twelve, just how experimental the plant had been, and that the desperate need of the material, caused by the war, meant that risks were taken that would, at any other time, have been totally unacceptable. From my experience later, I deduced that, if the plant was operating *now* in its original form, it would be closed down, immediately, by the Health and Safety Inspectorate, and those killed or injured, would have received massive compensation. As it was the widows received only small pensions.

The process essentially was to take ethylene, which is a gas at room temperature and highly flammable and compress it in large pressure vessels at a temperature of 160-170°C with the addition of catalysts such as benzaldehyde. These catalysts helped the ethylene to polymerise, converting it from a gas to the solid that we are all familiar with.

The main problem was that the pressure vessels had to operate at 1000-1900 ATS: that means, one thousand to nineteen hundred times the normal atmospheric pressure. They were in effect bombs waiting to go off. If there were any stray gases in the ethylene they could cause the mixture to explode.

Because the process was experimental it was difficult to control and regularly exploded. The explosions were heard even two miles away as a definite *Crump*! and were clearly recognisable.

Initially, until the engineers became wiser, they rebuilt the factory each time. Later, they realised that they didn't need a solid roof and designed one which was extremely light. This allowed the explosion to go upwards, straight into the air without any hindrance. The effect was to reduce the force of the explosion inside the factory and cause less damage to the plant and less harm to the workers. Some people were killed, but in view of the hazards, surprisingly few.

The constant proximity to danger caused instinctive responses. The effect on my father was, that, if anyone slammed a door suddenly or even banged something noisily, he would instinctively drop to the ground. Bang! Drop. It was quite simple.

Even after they built a new and improved plant at Wilton in Cleveland, they still hadn't perfected the process and explosions continued. Any large bang would produce the question, 'Was that the polythene plant?' People made jokes about it, but I've remember my dad's face turning grey when he heard that sound.

True to his word, Richard mentioned my problem to his wife and she told him to tell me that there was no way in which she could help, and I would do better to hand the gun in to the police and confess ignorance as to where it came from. I'd taken this advice to heart and was planning to do just that, when a day later I was handed an envelope. It had been left behind the bar at the club just addressed to:

Mr R. Foster Private and Confidential.
Inside there was just a short note which read:
Skipton Library 2/2/99 11:00 Economics section.

Chapter 14

I was intrigued but guessed who it was from. Tuesdays were when we usually played golf and Richard would be occupied. Of course, with my head injury, I had had to lay off golf for a while. Thus, on the appointed day I did just as instructed and wandered into the Skipton library situated at the top of the High Street by the Cenotaph just before 11:00.

The Economics Section was at the far end on the ground floor, virtually cut off from general view by the area dedicated to books on religion and politics – I never thought those two went together. This section was always quiet, and I thought what a suitable place to have a clandestine meeting.

I sat down and picked up an economics book entitled, *Keynsian Capital Flows*. After ten minutes of that stuff I was ready to escape and find a zoo to chat to the monkeys when suddenly Vera materialised. I had neither heard her approach nor come through the door. I almost jumped.

'Hi, Robert, fancy seeing you here,' she said. 'Aren't you playing today? I'm sure Richard is.' Flustered, I tried to think of a reply without implying that she'd sent the message.

'Oh…golf…no, my head. Hmm … I needed some info on … er… Tax law and just popped in.'

'But you're in the wrong section, that's upstairs. In the Reference Section. Come on, *chop-chop*, I'll show you.' With that she marched out with me following in her wake like a dog feeling a complete idiot. What was going on?

Upstairs was completely empty except for an assistant librarian, a young girl of perhaps seventeen with bright red hennaed hair tied up on the top of her head, and glasses with huge lenses. Without the glasses she would look like a coconut in the shy at the fairground, 'Three throws a shillin'.' they used to shout.

Vera sat herself down by a table at the far end of the room and gestured for me to do the same.

'Wasn't that fun, throwing the Russian spies off our scent?' she said and laughed, her eyes twinkling. My mouth was opening and shutting like a freshly landed carp. 'It just shows how ridiculous people can behave when they think that there's some secret or other. I was just having you on and you fell for the bait hook line and—'

'Sinker,' I muttered angrily.

'Now then, *what is your problem*, as they say?' she put her elbow on the table and her chin in her hand and looked at me with wide-open dark brown eyes and a big smile on her face.

My colour must have risen. I could feel myself getting hotter because she was treating me like a fool. I retorted,

'How was I supposed to know if it was *you* who'd written the note? If it wasn't I would have looked pretty damned ridiculous.'

'I didn't write it.'

'You must have, or else why are you here?'

'I didn't write it… I telephoned the bar at the club and Natalie wrote it down.'

'Oh, for God's sake,' I said exasperated and convinced that she was playing with me. 'You think I'm a complete idiot, don't you? Well forget I asked for your help …and Goodbye.' I stood up, feeling very angry.

'Sit down, Rob, for Heavens' sake and don't swear. I'm here now, aren't I? *And* I'm listening. I apologise, for teasing you. Don't take it so seriously. I know that you had an accident and a head injury. Sorry, and let me start again. You found a gun in your dad's effects?', she said sitting up.

Slightly mollified but still feeling annoyed, my head buzzing, I re-seated myself. I explained, yes, that I had unearthed a gun in my father's belongings and didn't know where it came from. I thought that she might be able to help in finding its origin, because of her war experiences.

'First of all, Rob, Richard and I were cross, that you, and presumably most of the club, knew that I was at 'that place'. Incredibly I noticed, or thought I did, that as she said 'that place' she lowered her voice a tad. '…But it was a long time ago.

I was at Oxford reading Classics and in 1942 there was a Daily Telegraph cryptic crossword competition which I entered. Apparently, it was a test by GC&CS (Government Code and Cipher School), which after the war became GCHQ (Government Communications Head Quarters); I passed and was accepted for you-know-where. I was nineteen and quite honestly my role was very minor. At first, I just listened to incoming radio signals and passed them on for deciphering; later on, I did do some deciphering myself. There's a lot of guff, you know, about what went on. Like most things in life, what seems exceptional and exciting, in practice, is dull, repetitive and boring. We thought more about young men and sex than how the war was going, and more about getting a pair of nylons than winning battles. Anyway, because we're friends I can speak frankly. Okay?' I nodded.

'It's highly unlikely that anyone now can trace the gun. Indeed, it is nigh on impossible to date it, except from archival records of any significant serial numbers. There are thousands out there you know. It might be from the First World War or the Second. More than likely it was a souvenir brought home by a soldier and sold on the black market, eventually landing up with your dad. It might even be a modern fake, a copy. Anyway, we've established that your dad had it and therefore obtained it somehow. Did he have a penchant for weapons and the like?'

'He had a standard issue 303 when he was in the Home Guard but that's all I know of. And when he was alive I never asked. So, what does that mean? Is that it? End of discussion?'

'No. I really want to help, and I must admit I like mysteries. By the way, do you have it with you?'

'Heck no, I am almost scared to touch it. As they say you never know where it's been.'

'Good, that was a joke you're improving. Right then, meet me here on Friday…here upstairs not downstairs, same time. And no need to come disguised.'

'You're doing it again!'

'Course I am, relax, it's fun."

'What about Richard? What does he think? Does he mind you doing this?'

'Oh, he thinks you're crazy and me for helping you. He's washed his hands of it. By the way, I'll not be alone. See you.' With that she whisked out of the swing doors and disappeared.

I couldn't make up my mind whether she was still pulling my leg, or she was just being practical and enjoying it. Richard had handled our affairs for a long time and he was justifiably annoyed only because he thought that Vera's past had become common knowledge. He was fair and straight to the point without bamboozling you with unnecessary jargon. If Vera wanted to waste her time on some wild goose chase, then it was her affair. Sally and I had met both of them at dances, particularly in our earlier years, but these had tended to be less and less as we got older. Our tastes changed, Sally with her W. I. and me golf. Of course, Vera played golf but had a greater interest in bridge which was not my cup of tea. She was an attractive blond with wavy hair now going platinum silver—and putting on a little weight. She was feisty and would tell you off even if you accidently miss-marked your ball on the green. I tended to avoid lady golfers like the plague. Now I had entered the dragon's den by enlisting her help. Bad move!

'Where have you been,' asked Sally.
'To the library looking at books on economics.'
'Now I know you're joking… economics, you can't even add up the shopping! Do you want a coffee, and do you fancy a hot cross bun?'
'"That would be great, but isn't it a bit early for hot cross buns?'
'They sell them at Christmas now. The seasons have all but disappeared. You know there's Easter eggs in Morrisons already.'
'Speaking of Easter. Is Shirley coming across?'
'Not sure. You know that Wane's got a heart problem well, apparently, it's flared up.'
'Oh, that's a pity.' It was always great to recap those heady days and nights in Winnipeg. I realised that I must tell Sally sometime but knew that she would just pooh-pooh the whole thing unless there were some concrete facts. She hadn't grown up in the bush, herding cattle with her father, brother and sister without dealing with life as it was, not *airy-fairy* things as they might be. Even though Sally had been in the GB for over forty years she still might revert and say,

'What a load of old cobblers… mate.'

Safely up in the exclusion zone of my study, I pondered my next move and thought, firstly, I would photograph the gun and the markings and, also, the piece of polythene with its incriminating microdots – including the magnified version. I realised that I hadn't mentioned this latter to anyone, including Vera. So be it. Let that be my little secret for now until I saw how things went.

This done I went up into the attic to find anything else that might have a bearing. Holding the little polythene aeroplane that was greenish in the subdued light in the attic I thought of the

Polythene Plant and, as though a light switch had been thrown, suddenly I was looking at it across the river.

I distinctly heard a voice,

'Yes'.

But I hadn't asked a question

1942

There were three of us, all aged about nine, the musketeers we called ourselves. We were yelling at two women in blue overalls, hair tightly tied up with scarves, who were illicitly smoking behind one of the buildings, part of the plant nearest to the river.

'Come on… throw us a ciggy.' To which they gave us what was, definitely, not a 'V' for victory sign.

The smell of the river was strong, mixed with that of the black foetid mud churned up by our feet. Partly hidden by the bulrushes we felt safe enough to torment them. It was also a good place to fish, particularly for perch - not that we ate them, they were too bony.

Between the River Weaver and the Trent and Mersey Canal was the Anderton Boat Lift. This marvellous invention lifted barges from the river up to the canal and vice versa with apparent ease, and to young boys, was magic. We would sit and watch or get into mischief if we could. On this occasion, there was an almost empty unattended barge. Almost empty although there were some coffee beans in the bottom; unattended because the bargees were at the local, *The Spinner*, just a few hundred yards away. Heaving myself over the side I scooped up a handful of the beautiful black shiny beads and climbed out again.

'If you smell them, they make your nose bleed,' said my youthful, and I thought, worldly-wise companion. I had never seen such wonderful looking things before, so I stuffed them into my hankie and pushed it into my trouser pocket - the one which wasn't torn. I had fallen from a fir tree when trying to collect a wood pigeon's egg and, as yet, my mother didn't know.

By myself later in the evening I took them out and, very warily, sniffed them, expecting at any moment a sudden rush of blood. The smell was disappointing, it was just like the Camp coffee my Gran made, but the beans were like jewels glistening in my hand.

The Polythene plant was located at Wallerscote, Winnington, at the river's edge on the other side of the River Weaver and nearly opposite to the boat lift. Being next to the River Weaver, there was always plenty of water to put out the fires which occurred It also meant that we could hide on the opposite bank in the rushes and observe what went on without ourselves being seen.

Why this should have been of interest to kids of eight or nine was simple. There were women, as well as men, working there, although the women were on the day shift only. And there were goings on.

We had had our education extended significantly by the comings and goings; the scuffling and the hurriedly rearranged clothing. Some of the blue overall-clad ladies were extremely fond of 'taking on' young male apprentices. Three or four would corner one and have his pants down, quick as a flash "just to have-a-look-see" and then run back inside the plant laughing.

We would hurl obscenities at anyone we saw, making certain not to be seen. When we shouted at the older women, however, they were shrewd and, since most of them came from Wincham, could make guesses as to who we were and would threaten to tell our mothers, yelling,

'We know who you are… just wait until we get our hands on you, you little buggers!' I think one of these was known as "Nellie Long Knickers".

Regaining the present in my study, I reflected that this Nellie Long Knickers lady was unique, at least in the sleepy little village of Higher Wincham. According to legend and in the close knit, knitting circles, she was greatly appreciated by the men folk of the village and at ICI. It did seem that she had had liaisons with quite a few of them. Certainly, in my mature years I had been told of the night that my dad and uncle were hauled out of the Red Lion by my aunt when it emerged that Nellie was on parade. This episode was told and retold like an epic and gathered its' own momentum each time. I have always imagined that the 'Long' came from the fact that they were often on show. She was unmarried and lived at No 7 Canal Lane in Boat Road. It was an address that I would not forget because one of my classmates had taken me home to next door, No.8. The living room which you entered from the road was tiny. It was spotlessly clean, but I was intrigued by the newspaper on the table instead of a tablecloth. On it were some cups and some glasses. My school friend saw me looking at the glasses and said proudly,

'Them's milk bottles cut down.'

He went on to explain how his dad heated up the bottle on the range and then carefully laying it down dropped a little water half way down so that the water ran around, and the bottle split cleanly into two halves. The bottom half made a perfect glass.

Now, what was most interesting to me was that I had *consciously* thought of the Polythene Plant and, as it were, went there, as a boy. To experiment I tried to think of Yarby Plastics, where I had worked, but with no great success. I could remember incidents, but they were just memories. Obviously there had to be greater emotions in play to be transported as it were. The experiment was however promising.

I began to search through more of my Dad's old papers. As I noted earlier, the notebooks were heavily taped with the now brittle Sellotape which had gone a dark brown, so much so that you could not read through it. Then I had a thought. With one of my photographic programmes you could restore old yellowed photos to the original black and white. It was almost like magic. I thought it would be worth trying to see if it would clean up my dad's notes. I took the first book, which was a record of his weekly wages from 1938. It worked. First, I photographed the page then saved it and then used the Adobe Photoshop programme to clean up and restore its original colour. In clear black and white, there were his written entries.

Having been successful, I tried the rest of the book, but each page was the same, just records of wages. Another book, when treated, yielded something much more puzzling. Just rows of dots on graph paper which my Dad had pasted in.

Chapter 15

1999 Friday 5th February

I told Sally that I had to go to the library to look at some plant books to which she retorted. 'If it gets you into the garden that'll be great.' I let it go because to have entered into any discussion would have blown my rather shaky deception.

I went upstairs to the reference section as arranged and waited. At eleven-ten, I started to fidget. At eleven thirty, I was ready to leave when in breezed Vera with a tall, white-haired man of, I guessed, about eighty-five. He was wearing a grey topcoat and a trilby and walked with a slight limp. He carried a briefcase in his right hand and a silver topped cane in the other. Not bad as a description to give to the police, I thought. He looked official.

'Rob, I would like to introduce you to an old friend of mine. Call him William, it's not his real name but it will do. William, this is Robert Foster.' As I shook William's hand she addressed herself to him, clearly for my benefit.

'I explained to you what Robert had found, and you kindly agreed to see whether it could be traced.' Then to me,

'I assume that you've brought it with you, Rob?'

'Yes, and it's inside the original box I found it in.' I said and gave him the box. He put it in his briefcase without even checking it and then, taking off his trilby, sat down. Vera and I followed suit opposite him.

'You understand that now I have it, it will not be returned,' said William. 'I will see that it enters the graveyard for old weapons, and there will be no questions asked by the authorities.'

My face fell,

'I didn't realise that you would keep it.' I said lamely.

'The problem is, Robert, you don't mind if I call you Robert, do you?' I shrugged. 'That it is an illegal weapon and, normally, I would have to inform the police ... Should I continue?'

Vera interrupted., You do know, Robert, that you cannot possess a gun without a licence?' Somewhat chastened and, feeling like a schoolboy who has transgressed some rule and been sent to the headmaster's study, I tried to regain some dignity,

'Of course, I understand, and accept. What happens now?'

'I will do my best, as I promised Mrs Bowden, to trace it and see whether it has form.'

'What do you mean 'form'?

'Whether it has been used in any crimes and so on.'

'My God, I hadn't thought of that,' I said, wondering whether I should just have chucked the damned gun into the Trent and Mersey, or the Rylston duck pond.

'Don't worry, as I said, there will be no repercussions, I promise you. Is there anything else you would like to tell me?'

'About what?'

'Anything.'

Oh, there's a faint mark in the magazine, I think it's a letter 'z', faint but visible. Did I mention this to you? I said addressing Vera

'I don't think so,' she replied but I noticed that there was a quick exchange of glances between her and William. You did say a 'Z'?'

'Yes, I think so.' I replied.

'Well, in that case I'll be off. Good day to you.' Putting on his trilby he doffed it to us and was gone.

'What happens now?' I asked Vera the same question.

'As far as he is concerned he'll do his part and let me know what has been found. Then I'll let you know and we can take it from there. Did you really think that you could have kept the gun?'

'Actually, I hadn't thought about it at all. Except that I took photos of it just for my records – out of habit I guess. Is that it for you?'

'How do you mean?'

'Have you no further interest?'

'Why, do you have something else?' I could sense that she was still interested and apparently keen to dig further. I decided that I would take her into my confidence and tell her about the books.

'Actually, you might be of greater help with something other than the gun. My father left several notebooks. Most are just a record of his wages, but one is in code.'

'Ah, so now you think I'm a code breaker?' That lovely cheeky smile appeared and softened her apparent challenge.

'I didn't know what you were, and I'm not sure what you are even now, but I'm guessing that you have a talent. Am I correct?'

All right I confess. I'm hooked. I love solving puzzles.'

'So, you'll help?'

'Yep, of course I'll give it a go.'

'When shall "we three meet again" then … an' all that?'

'There won't be a next time for the three of us. 'William' won't appear again, he's only doing this for my sake. His work, when he was in harness, was *dark and deep.*'

'Dark and deep!' I said what's that supposed to mean?'

It means that he used to work in areas of deep shadows. I never knew more than a tip of it, even though for a short time he was my boyfriend.'

'Wow! Your boyfriend? Does Richard know?'

'Yes and no, and that's as much as I'm going to tell *you.*'

'Fair enough. So, next Friday?'

'Yes, that sounds good…in the meantime maybe see you on the course.'

Chapter 16

When I was a boy I used to listen avidly to Dick Barton, Special Agent. This investigation was starting to appear to be as whacky as a radio script. I thought, what had Vera said?' *William* was *Deep and dark*!

Oh God! I'm suddenly in an inky darkness with just a narrow beam of light illuminating wet and slimy walls, and water dripping onto my head and shoulders. The air, which I gasped, was humid and smelled of prehistory.

I realised I was underground and clinging onto a rope ladder for dear life. My foot slipped, and a shot of adrenaline whizzed through my body.

'Jesus, I yelled and swung myself back to regain my footing on the rung. I paused for a second to get my breath back, my heart thudding. Then, I resumed my climb once more, prompted by a tug on the rope and yells from up top,

'Rob ... you okay? You stopped.'

'Yes, I'm fine... I was just taking a rest.'

'Well, if you feel like a sleep, just let me know,' came the impatient reply from Jimmy our guide.

I remembered we were doing Alum Pot on Simon Fell; above were Kevin and Sadie, below were Alan and John. But I didn't need this, I wanted to be out of this dream or flashback, or whatever the hell it was. Out, out I thought.

And just as easily as that, I was. I was back in my study. What had brought that on? Perhaps mention of deep and dark had triggered something. Also, I had willed myself out of the dream, or whatever it was. I felt this was more progress.

I wanted to be able to control my comings and goings. But what about the other flashbacks? What had triggered those. I felt this was important. Perhaps I could control where and when I went. I tried to think of somewhere, but my mind just flittered about. I had mental images but not any presence. In other words, I wasn't actually there. The phrase *ich war dabei* came up, but nothing happened. I remembered the wall and all the festivities of that night but now it was just that… only a memory. I tried thinking of something big…the Eiffel tower, that was big, and I saw it, but it was just as in a postcard. Taj Mahal, again, the well-known image. I knew that it should be all pink in the early morning light, but I couldn't see the pinkness. I couldn't smell the heady smells of spices and dust, in other words the smells of India. That was a bit daft, I thought, thinking of that, you've never even been there.

'Would you like a cup of coffee,' came from below.

'Yes, I'd love one, thanks, Sally.'

Dear old Sally, I thought, not as she was now but when she was a beautiful eighteen.

The fire was roaring, and pine logs were sparking and spitting in the large open fireplace. Outside the temperature might have been minus twenty but inside the small bedroom and inside these furs, snuggling naked next to Sally, it was hot. I tensed. Sally stirred and hugged me closer. One eye opened,

'I love you Robbie. Wasn't that wonderful? Was it as good for you?' she asked anxiously, looking up at me. My hands stroked her back which had a thin film of perspiration on it; her slim young body moulding into mine.'

'It was fantastic…God, it was wonderful!' I replied.

She smiled and reburied her head under the furs, her tangled blond hair spreading out like a halo above them. Her voice came from underneath, muffled and sadder.

'But what now, Rob? If we want to be together like this again, there's nowhere to go and, in any case, you're due to go back to England next month.'

'We'll think of something my love, just let's enjoy this whilst we can.' My mind was buzzing and examining alternatives when I realised that someone was shouting but that couldn't be, we were alone. Oh hell! Had our weekend triste been rumbled? The shouting grew.

'It's a new brand from somewhere up in the Andes, Alta Rica. Hello! Anybody in there? Are you asleep?'

'What... we'll be okay, something will turn up,' I replied dreamily.'

I yearned to get back to the log cabin and the smell of pine logs burning and whatever pheromones we were emitting.

'What'll turn up? It might be the postman. Who else were you expecting to turn up?' Sally had, unnoticed by me, entered the study and plonked a cup of coffee on my desk.

'Blinking and grasping for time I opened my eyes and focussed on the cup then grasped it and slurped at my coffee. Damn, it was hot! That brought me back to reality in a flash. Sally was old again. This time I knew that Sally had been with me in that cabin too, so I could ask her a question.

'Sally' I said, 'I know it sounds daft but do you remember *that* weekend we had in your uncle's cabin at Twin Lakes' Beach ?

'Do I remember! You're joking; how could I forget where Jackie was conceived? What made you think of that? You're not getting all sentimental in your old age, are you?'

'No, I was trying to remember something. Did we drink coffee?'

'Holy moly! What a question to ask after all these years. *Did we drink coffee*? Not as I remember ...you probably gave me vodka to get me drunk. Remember, I was a young, innocent virgin ... all alone, and all the way from the colonies. No, come to think of it I think all we had was beer. What a strange man you are sometimes. Was it me talking about coffee that brought it on? Anyway, just to tell you I'm off into town to do some shopping. You haven't forgotten that Bill and Mary are coming round tonight?'

'Oh, my God. Yes, I had.'

'Too much daydreaming that's what it is. You know sometimes you remind me of the young abos we used to have on the ranch, when they went walk-about.'

After she'd left a sudden thought struck me. *If* I could go back in time, why not go back and try to stop that accident to mother's spine. Maybe I could put that ten shilling note back on the sideboard? What would happen then? Maybe no back problem, different life. But how? I tried hard to concentrate. Think of New Brighton; think of running to get to the cinema. Yes, I could remember it, but it wasn't the same, it was just a memory. I couldn't get back. Think of mother in the church getting her leg burned. It was the same. I couldn't see the scene at all clearly. I remembered, logically, that they were in the clothes of the period, like black and white photos but there was no colour. Before there had been colours, browns and greens and even a purply-pink. These had gone. Before, I could smell the stale sweat, earthy smells, and the perfume worn by her mother. I remembered it was Lily of the Valley, but I couldn't smell anything now. I looked at my leg, the red mark had disappeared.

It was as though the flashback was used up. It was now just a memory. Weird.

Chapter 17

1999 Friday 12th February

'Why are we meeting here?' I said. There were just the two of us, even the librarian had disappeared, perhaps realising that we were not here to steal any books. Before she left she had whispered to Vera,

'If you need anything I'm just downstairs.' Did I look like a dangerous villain not to be trusted?

'Where *did* you want to meet then?' Vera said in a teasing sort of tone. 'It's warm, you can get a cuppa if you wish. I don't think Richard would like us to meet at home, he likes his privacy. How about Sally?' Now I felt on the defensive.

'I haven't actually told her that we're meeting,' I said lamely.

'Then I'll tell her. What've you got to hide? I told you this business about secrets is a load of rubbish. In any case all you've just asked me to help you with is to find out about that gun.' I felt that I was getting deeper into trouble. She was pushing me.

'I haven't told her about the gun either. She'd only worry.'

'Oh lord, I think that bang on the head did more than just raise a lump.'

'I had ten stitches and an operation, it wasn't just a lump you know,' I retorted. 'I'll tell her…tonight,' I added. She was at it again teasing me, challenging. 'So then, what've you got to tell me.'

'Not much—'

'Then why *are* we here?' I snapped now cross.

'Hang on, hang on …' She said, 'don't be so impatient. I just said *not much*… I didn't say 'nothing', or is that correct? Because that means I did say 'something' …'

'Please. Can't you just get on with it?' She leaned forward to deliver her news. She was looking directly at me, watching my face, waiting for what she knew had to be a huge reaction. As she talked my mouth dropped further and further open.

'The Luger serial number 7431 was issued in 1936 to one Heinrich Zeissmann, Abwehr Section II. That particular section was indirectly under the control of the spy-master, Admiral Canaris. For a stupid reason, probably, bravado, Zeissmann, scratched the tiny z in the magazine, which sort of confirms it.

Zeissmann studied at Oxford in 1930-34, reading for a BSc specialising in Chemistry. After he obtained his degree he returned to Germany and spent some time in Bavaria, we believe, in a clandestine section training agents in espionage. Then we lost track of him. He disappeared in 1938 never to be seen or heard of since.'

All this was delivered by Vera as though she was reading a weather report, ignoring the disbelief registering on my face. She leaned back with a triumphant smile.

'What! You must be joking!' I managed to gasp. If she'd told me that they had just confirmed that the world was flat after all, it would come as less of a shock.

'Yes, it's true and please close your mouth, Rob, it makes you look older. That's right, it's been confirmed, incontrovertibly, that Zeissmann was trained as a German spy before World War II. It's not a secret now. And it's a fact that the gun …your gun …was issued to him. William, probably, got the info from the German Interior Ministry. What's not known is how your Dad got hold of it. Shall I go and get us a coffee whilst you think about it?' She smirked, I could have smacked her, then changed my mind. I grovelled.

'Bloody hell! Oh…er…sorry. Yes, thanks…er…please. I'm sorry I bit your head off. I seem to lose my patience more easily these days.'

'It's no problem…Bye…I'll be back.' She smiled and disappeared to get the coffee.

Now I had more questions than I could cope with. The luger, which had been in my dad's possession had been issued to a German spy. Did I believe Vera? Of course I did. Why would she tell me a falsehood? If I did believe her, then how could my Dad have got hold of it? Surely then, it wasn't just a random souvenir from a pub? That would seem to be too much of a coincidence. Firstly, there was the gun *and* then what appeared to be microdots in a piece of polythene. I came back to what I had wondered originally. Could the history of the gun be in any way connected to the Polythene plant? I was more certain now and felt that my gut feeling could be correct. I was in way over my head. My other question was, were the flashbacks also connected and, if so, how and why?

'Here you are,' Vera reappearing said brightly, as though she was at a WI coffee morning. 'Two Café Lattes. Or should that be Cafés Latte? No forget that, I'm being pedantic. Okay? Let me tell you what has happened. William - I did tell you it's not his real name – was able to discover when and where the gun had been registered, it was apparently quite easy. Do you remember that there were serial numbers on the gun – or did you even notice?

'Yes, I did notice them, but they were very faint.'

Well, obviously, with the right techniques William and his colleagues were able to decipher them. The next task was to find out if the gun had been used in any crime in the UK and Europe etc. So, the details were sent to Interpol. The data files showed, or rather confirmed, that there were no reported incidents involving the gun i.e. no crimes on record anywhere. There was not a single record of it since it was issued. However, because its use had been first registered in Germany officials of the Federal Ministry of Justice (under the War Weapons Control Act) requested its return to them to run further tests and carry out research for their archives. So, it has gone, and William is out of it. There will be no follow up; no embarrassing questions as to how your father obtained it. And for that matter why you broke the law.

I had learned my lesson not to interrupt her and listened quietly like a little schoolboy. I felt like saying *yes ma'am no ma'am, three bags full ma'am*. Part of me also understood that I could have been in some trouble and, therefore, I should be grateful for what she had accomplished and so quickly.

Although at seventy-five she was a little on the matronly side I realised that she must have been an absolute stunner when she was younger. Even now, her brown eyes were slightly dilated and dancing with excitement as she talked. She was obviously loving the chase, a challenge, possibly not encountered since those wartime days. A lot better than the weekly golf medal. She was in her stride now and not to be stopped. My assumptions were proved to be correct when she continued.

'Here and now, Bob, I'm expressing my interest and *am* willing to work with you to find out more from your dad's side and what it signified. *But*, there are certain conditions.' As she paused, I understood that I needed to reply. Her tone was now more schoolma'am-ish, which quelled my more romantic thoughts about her and her past like a dose of ice-water.

'Pardon? Conditions?'

'Yes, if I'm to help you, I want your promise that firstly, no book will be written without my express permission and, secondly, there will be no disclosure of any sort to the media, involving me, any of my family or colleagues. Third, Sally and Richard will be told, but no one else. Okay?'

I think that it was the way she said it, which for some reason, re-ignited my anger. I didn't know why but I was not okay. In fact, I was most decidedly *not okay*. I was blazing with anger.

'Get out... get out you blasted quack, or I'll break every bone in your blasted body!
"But I was asked to come, just to see if I could help.'
'The only help you'll get is a kick up the arse... Now get out of here. Go. Now!'
I had just got back home from my night shift and I see that this damned bone manipulator is in the sitting room with Alice, doing something to her back and she's yelling for him to stop. If he comes again I'll kill him. I put my arms round her shoulders.
'He won't come again, I promise you...'

'Rob ... Robert. Are you all right?' The anxious question penetrated my blood red haze. 'Are you okay? Rob look at me.' Then once more darkness descended.
I'm cold, so cold; the mere is deep and I'm only half way across. I can't go back, it's just as far. Just keep the rhythm going, left arm over right, right arm over left. It's a damned silly thing to do. No one asked you to do this; no one even had a bet with you: it's just your own stupid idea, something you felt you must do. Wriggle your toes to stop getting cramp. The water's so black out here ... underneath are all those bream and pike - like the one my dad caught in a bucket - and eels. Oh, it's so cold. Left arm over right, right arm over left ...breathe ... left arm over ...

The lights of the reading room came flooding back. I was so cold, I shuddered. Then I gasped, as though for breath and tried to stand up. Vera was holding me by the shoulders helping me to get up and looking anxiously into my eyes. I managed to slide onto the chair with Vera still supporting me.

'Rob … just sit still… you fainted, or something. It was weird. Here, have a drink of your coffee. She pushed the cup into my hands and raised it to my lips. There, is that better?'

The coffee was hot and strong, and the caffeine seemed to speed through my veins. I looked round. The room was just as it had been. Vera still had her arm on my shoulder. Just then the door opened and the young woman, the librarian, came in.

'I heard shouting, is everything all right? She looked anxious, almost afraid, as though her suspicions had been confirmed that I was a dangerous lunatic.

'Yes, thanks, everything is okay.' Vera replied calmly and firmly. 'My friend just had a touch of cramp that's all.' Even in my confused condition I thought you lie very easily, Mrs Bowden.

'Oh, if you're sure…' said the librarian and exited.

'Now then. Tell me what the hell just happened?' demanded Vera. 'One minute you are with me, then the next you are yelling about the cold and not getting cramp and before that flailing your arms and threatening to kill someone.'

Feeling more certain and less confused, the coffee had helped. And, I was becoming more used to these events said,

'I'm know I'm Robert Foster, but just a few moments ago I swear I was my father.'

'That's stupid. Your father's *dead*, you said so yourself, Vera protested. I could see that she was exasperated but, at the same time, worried. It was understandable for her to believe that my injury had made me unstable, possibly even dangerous, and it was coming across as anger.

'I know it doesn't make any sense.' I replied shakily. Will you just give me a moment, please, to think it through?'

This last episode made my mind up. I realised that I had to tell someone what was happening, and it might as well be Vera. Tell her *everything* I told myself, particularly if she was going to help me.

Chapter 18

'Vera, please sit down, I'm okay now, and I'll try to explain. You said you wanted to know everything. Well that may take quite a long time, but I will try to go over it bit by bit. Please be patient. First let me have another drink of coffee.' Now it was my turn to talk and hers to listen. Even that idea made me feel better.

'Since that injury to my head I have been having lapses...sort of flashbacks. I had a couple just now.'

Vera interrupted. 'Flashbacks? What do you mean? Do you mean memories of things that happened in your past?'

'Yes and no. More than just memories, sometimes. Please let me continue and try to hold your questions until I've finished.'

I told her that immediately after the injury to my head I started to have these – for want of a better word – flashbacks. They started with my very early memories as a young child, playing in the fields and seeming to be in the field; *being* in our house, its rooms, the wallpaper and the green distemper; the garden: not just remembering but *experiencing* the sensation of hot and cold. I could smell the grass in the fields - I even experienced hay fever, which as a young child I used to get. Later I *saw*, or *was*, my mother in church, our village church in Wincham when she was six or seven. In other words, the year must have been around 1916 -17 and I wasn't even born. I could smell them, stale and sweaty. I could see the colours of clothing they - and she, *or I* - was wearing. She burned her leg and I felt it. The burn even raised a mark on my own leg. Are you following?'

Vera looked at me, 'I'm hearing what you are saying but I don't understand it at all. Anyway, please carry on and I'll ask questions later.' She said this calmly, but I could tell that she was now classifying the information into possible, probable, and lunatic. I nevertheless continued.

I mentioned the fact that some of the things *could* have been memories just trawled up, but others could *not* have been. For example, my mother feeding the pigs and talking to her elder sister—.'

'Yes, but you'd probably heard her, or someone speak of these things,' said Vera, interrupting. Obviously, she couldn't help herself. I shook my head and put my hand up to silence her.

'Please hear me out. In this last episode, I was swimming in a mere. probably Marbury, or Marston in Cheshire. I've never done that, I would never have the courage. I hate the thought of getting tangled up in weeds. I felt cold and frightened, but it wasn't *my* fear; it was my father's. That other recent one was when somebody, probably a chiropractor, was treating my mother at home. I'd heard about the incident, but it was my dad who was angry, not me and I saw everything through my dad's eyes and ears and heard, whoever it was, that my dad threw out. At other times it was clearly me in the flashback. Just as weird, I even thought that I came home from hospital *twice*. The worst is that I feel that there's some purpose to all this, but I don't know what it is. My mother didn't die. So, why would I dream that she did. My father was not killed by a bomb, it's all fantasy. But is it? Is there something that I'm missing, something I should do? If there is, what is it?

'Don't you think that it all stems from that injury to your head? Maybe you should see the consultant again. Do more tests.'

'You're probably right. But what about this last one? Might it have had anything to do with what you told me? That my dad had the gun of a known spy. I mean you realise that it was a huge shock.'

'I've no idea about these things but I suppose it's possible. I was cock-a-hoop, being naughty, because I realised I had such dramatic news. The way I told it was *meant* to be dramatic, to give you a shock. I'm truly sorry for that, if *that* caused the hallucination. And, if it did, perhaps we should stop. Do you want to stop?'

'No, I'm okay now and I want to find out how my dad came to have that Luger and if there is anything more about it that you know.'

'I've told you everything that I was told. I can ask William whether there was anything else, but it seemed that what was known about the spy Zeissmann came to a dead end. The last year that he was known to be alive was in 1938. Maybe it was just that, maybe he was killed?'

'I understand and thanks for everything you have done so far. But what I really want to know was whether it had anything to do with the Polythene Plant at Walllerscote.' This was the moment I figured to tell her about the other things I had found, but I didn't want anyone else to know.

'There is something else, but I would like what I am about to tell you to be our secret, at least for the time being. Okay, you can give a hint to Richard, but I am getting into things which are very personal. So, can you agree to that?' I was putting her on the back foot now. She had to agree to keep quiet, and I could see her mulling it over. Then she smiled,

'Well, as long as it's legal and won't hurt anyone, I suppose that's okay. So yes. I'm not sure that I'm ready for any more shocks but go on.'

'In amongst my father's things is a toy aeroplane made of a luminous polythene - in other words it shines in the dark—'

'I do know what luminous means, for God's sake!' Vera retorted. 'But go on.'

'I know that you know, but I wanted to make the point because I remember playing with this as a child, in my bath with the light off. But to continue, I also found a chip of polythene about three inches square, a sort of retained production quality sample dated 21st December 1940.'

'Right. Those things are pretty normal, I suppose. Who would normally keep them?'

'Oh,' I answered, irritably, because she was interrupting my news. 'Normally, they would be kept by the quality control laboratory, but that's not the point. The point is that this innocent chip of polythene would have been a timebomb in 1940, when the process was secret.' I paused. Vera waited.

'It has microdots … embedded in it!'

It was her turn to be taken aback. The ramblings of a benign madman were acceptable, and she was well aware that I'd been injured, and that could be the reason why I could be dreaming weird dreams and having hallucinations. The gun could still most likely have been picked up in a pub, and it was merely coincidental that it had belonged to a known spy before or during WWII. But, *microdots* didn't grow on trees and, if what I had said was correct, they came from a piece of plastic with a known source. All this I could see went through her mind in a flash.

'*You are joking?*' she said wide-eyed.

'No, I'm not joking. And I'll prove it. You see, now it's my turn to surprise *you*.' I took the plastic sample out of a little polythene container in which I had kept it and gave it to her (the irony of it being in a Tupperware box didn't escape me and made me smile). Then I gave her my piece glass. She peered through the powerful little magnifier and her head almost touched the table as she looked even closer and moved it over the dots,

'Cripes! I can't see much but there's something there all right. This puts it into another category altogether.

'Well then, take a look at these.' I said handing her the photos I had taken of the enlargements I had made.

'Oh Wow! Now I can see they're full of figures ... Data!'

'That's right.' I said, almost smirking, but relieved that I had now shared the information with someone. Something was telling me that I was doing the right thing.

'What do *you* know about microdots?' she asked me.

'Nothing, I had to look them up on Wikipedia to find out anything about them. What about you?'

'Only in James Bond films and old whodunits. It wasn't my area of speciality.'

'Well, from what I have gathered, to start with, you need a very special camera, which takes a one mm, image. Then to read the microdot, you place it on the end of special lens or, of course, a microscope. But what I *am* sure of is that you don't just point a camera and click. It must take a lot of organisation and these plans must have come from an office or laboratory and, you have to have an idea of what you are looking for.' I said.

'I agree,' she replied, looking at me in an altogether different way. Finally, she decided,

'Okay, I'm suitably impressed and intrigued, and I want to follow it up. Now, do you remember… when I asked you who would have kept these, you told me the lab. Well, doesn't that suggest the person who made these worked in the laboratory. And would have access to the samples and, possibly, the plan of the works.'

'By God you're right. I didn't make that connection,' I said, again suitably impressed at the speed with which she could take something in and run with it.

'Ok, do you think it might be a good idea if we take a break now?' she asked. Perhaps you can do some more research and I can poke around discretely. Then in a few days I can come to your house - because that's where your dad's records are - and we can see what else we can discover?'

'Yes, I agree,' I said, nodding. 'I'm sure we'll find more answers if there are two heads - maybe that should be three counting my two! That's if Sally agrees, of course.'

'Absolutely. How about next Friday, Fridays are good for me?'

'Agreed, and this gives us both time to put down more details on paper. But can we make it Friday week? I've got an appointment with a trick cyclist on Friday.' She laughed, 'that doesn't surprise me in view of what you have told me.'

In a way I felt that telling Vera had relieved some of the tension in my head. I felt calmer, a problem shared... I didn't tell Sally about the microdots but tried to tell her what I'd been experiencing, including the sudden flashbacks or visions from the past, omitting, because it didn't seem relevant, that remembered weekend in Winnipeg, which I hadn't mentioned to Vera either. As expected, Sally just laughed,

'You're a silly old codger that's what you are. All this nonsense about spies and guns. Anyway, you say the gun is gone and the police aren't involved so, if it keeps you busy, I'm happy. I like Vera so there isn't a problem about her coming here. It sounds as though I'd better make sure we have lots of coffee.'

I thought that's just so typical of Sally. I'm telling her about my Dad's involvement in possible international espionage and she wants to make sure she doesn't run out of coffee - and I'll bet she'll get some extra biscuits... I retired to my haven, my study, and tried to organise my thoughts by making notes:

<u>Fact:</u> the gun my dad had, belonged *at some time*, to a spy called <u>Zeissmann.</u>
Did he work at ICI? Did he work in the Polythene Plant? Did he work in the lab?
<u>Don't have answers.</u>

<u>Fact</u>: my dad had a chip of polythene dated 21st December 1940 with microdots showing details of an industrial plant.
Was it the polythene plant?
<u>Don't know</u>, but it was more than likely.
Where did it come from?
<u>Don't know,</u> but my Dad had it and kept it.

Only further research could determine answers to the *don't knows*. No amount of research, though, could tell me why I witnessed my father chasing a quack out of our house. Another don't know, but there seemed to be a causal link to high emotion and mother. A lot of my previous dreams, illusions, delusions, hallucinations, or whatever, had been concerned with my mother. Now, it seemed my father was trying to invade my thoughts. Why?

At times, I was transported back in time i.e. *my* memory time, that is, about things I had experienced; and in others I was in someone else's time and memory.

As yet, I could not choose a time, or place. It just happened. A word, a smell, and in the last episode, a shock. Yes, that was certainly a clue, a clear link to emotions: anger, joy, love, guilt, fear, hate, loathing...lust even! When I tried to manage a memory, however, it was just a postcard memory.

In the meantime, I decided to get out all the photos and documents from the boxes which my dad had left. I'll bet my mother still has some, but they could only be few because we sorted things when she moved to Robin Hood's Bay. I must check though.

According to his birth certificate my father was born in Marsham on the 31st of January 1912, or was he? I remembered something about there being a doubt about the date. That might be a start.

Digging through the piles of wills, birth and death certificates, I unearthed a letter from my Grandfather William Foster to the Home Secretary Reginald McKenna dated April 12th, 1912 (he had succeeded Winston Churchill the year before). The handwritten letter was, most probably, a copy of the original, but whether the original was typewritten or not was unknown. It states that due to my Grandfather's illness – of which I knew nothing – there had been a mistake on my father's birth certificate and that he was, actually, born on the January 30th not the 31st. I couldn't trace a reply and thought it quite possible that none was sent since the Home Secretary had more important things on his hands, for example, fighting against Churchill's plan to build a new Mediterranean fleet. My guess was that this letter was just buried. I remembered my mother joking that my dad never knew what day it was but hadn't thought to ask for details. I came back to the book in which there were dots and squiggles. What could they mean? I needed Vera.

'You're going to need more room than in your study, said Sally. Why don't you lay them out in the box-room?' She could see that I was getting into a mess with photos here, and piles of papers overflowing onto the floor. There's nothing much in there and it can soon be cleared.'

'What would I do without you,' I murmured, thinking just how much of my life she was beginning to organise, maybe she sensed, now that I was getting older that her time was coming.

'Thank you dear,' I said.

Chapter 19

Friday 19th March

'Okay, where shall I start, said Vera.

We were in the box-room, with the photos and documents spread over the bed and window sills, which, being nearly three feet deep were very useful.

'Coffee or tea?' shouted Sally from the stairs.

'Tea's fine … milk no sugar.'

'Yorkshire Gold okay?'

'That's my favourite,' replied Vera loudly.

'Er…I'll have coffee please.' I said, butting in, because I seemed to have been deemed irrelevant, and written out of the script.

'And biscuits?' once more, from Sally halfway down the stairs.

'Yes please,' we both yelled in unison.

'Would you take a look at these photo-enhanced copies of the pages from his notebook, the ones with the oddly spaced dots.' I said. She buried her head almost to the page. She's short sighted, I thought, even though she was wearing glasses. I had seen this before in the office. I had the opposite problem. Before I had glasses, I was holding letters at arms-length trying to focus.

'Have you got such a thing as a perpetual calendar?' asked Vera.

'A what?'

'A calendar, when you can see what day it was for any date from 1800 to 2050.'

'No.'

'Well, download one, I think it'll be useful.' Yes, ma'am I thought, two bossy women. Good job the girls aren't home, I'd be demented.

Vera studied the perpetual calendar and started to work through the printed and improved copies of the original. Here and there she inserted dates and, I think, times. I went back into my study and copied some more of the entries, taking them to Vera who laid them out in order. She broke off to advise me.

'Just as I thought. These dots are groups of dates, days, and possibly times. Did your dad possibly work shifts? She asked pertly.

'Bloody Hell, that was quick! Of course, he did, I thought. 'They worked a three-shift system, you know, six-two; two-ten and ten-six.'

'No, that doesn't fit. Oh, and you're swearing again. Please don't, it distracts me. Did he work twelve-hour shifts at all?'

'Of course, he did. I'm stupid. During the war, twelve-hour shifts were quite common, you know - even for women.'

'Then that's it. These are shift patterns. By the way, I do know about the war; and for your information, women at Bletchley regularly worked twelve-hour shifts-including nights and even longer hours when there was a flap on.'

'I'm sorry, I keep forgetting; it's because you look so… er—'

'You mean well preserved?'

'No, now you're teasing again. I find it difficult to imagine you as a young woman and—'

'Give it up, mate, you're digging the hole deeper,' she said and laughed.

'Sorry. So is that all that they are, his shift times?' I felt disappointed that they did not represent anything more mysterious.

'Well, that's what they seem to be at first sight, but there are some places where the dots are slightly bigger or more pronounced. Does that give you any clue?'

'None that I can think of.'

'They could be accidental but I'm not sure of that. What I will do is to record all the dates and times and print them in a slightly different order as a table, so they will be easier to follow. Then we could see whether those with larger dots mean anything. What do you know about 'sets'?'

'Eh? What sort of sets? wireless sets? headsets…?'

'Never mind, I will explain as I go along. It's code work. Let's get these onto your computer in the order I have written them down. Then print them.

'*Jewohl mein Fuhrer*,' I said and gave her a heil salute.

'Ok, okay, I should have said *please*,' she said sighing. 'Men don't like being bossed by women do they?'

'Thank you, and no.'

'Then do as you're told,' she flashed a great big smile at me. 'You know I'm loving this.'

It was great working with Vera. Even without knowing what she had done during the war, you could sense her intellect. Eyes shining, everything focussed on the problem, she almost had an aura. This energy was never shown on the golf-course, I suppose because she did not wish to stand out.

I wondered what she would have done without the war, the frenetic excitement of Bletchley Park. Finished her degree, done a Masters, then what? Teaching? I couldn't envisage her as a history teacher, trying to drum the names and dates of the Kings and Queens of England circa 1066-1953 into a class of acne-laden fourth form boys. Or, as the French Mistress, intoning irregular verbs, to a class of glazed-eyes fifth form girls. Maybe, she would have become a civil servant and finished up in the Treasury, or the Foreign Office; certainly, I could not see her in the dull-as-dishwater Home Office.

I would love to have met her as a twenty-year old but realised that, even as a contemporary, she would have been out of my class.

Cambridge v Manchester Tech: one-nil! Ah, well, I thought, I'm glad she's here now.

We continued the work with Vera dictating more dates and times and sometimes, as instructed, I used the star key instead of a dot.

'This was part of my work, eventually.' Vera said. 'It was a case of finding patterns and then cracking messages which were in code; like solving crossword puzzles.' When I had finished printing all the sheets she shooed me away and started to examine them.

As she beavered away, I sorted through, and tried to identify people in the photographs. Only a few were marked with names. So often that link is broken because those who knew who was in the photograph and where and when it was taken, have died. When the photographs were new there was no need to label them because someone, a family member, or friend, would be able to fill in the details. Recently, my mother had tried to put names to images but, even she, had identified one of me as a toddler as my brother.

Vera broke off scrutinising the lists and came to look. 'So that's your dad?' she asked, pointing at my father with some of my mother's brothers, obviously they were on some outing in the summer, probably round about 1930 or 1931. There was no information as to where it was taken, but it could have been a local fête. He had a straw boater on his head adjusted to a jaunty angle. Another was of my dad in a group of middle-aged men, probably workmates or colleagues, taken in the '60s at Wilton, possibly Wilton Castle, the administration centre for the petrochemical complex. Obviously, this photo had been taken after my father, and two uncles, together with their families, relocated to Cleveland following the move of the industry.

'And what's this one.' Vera said holding up a folded newspaper clipping. She opened it out.

'Ah, that's the photo taken of a German bomber which was shot down at Winsford, 'I said. 'Actually, I kept this cutting because it shows the plane and standing nearby, bizarrely, is my Uncle Ron, Auntie Vicky's husband.

I didn't see the photograph when it was first published in the Northwich Guardian, which as you can see was dated the 12th June 1940, but I saw it a few years later when it was re-issued. I remembered that the whole school was taken to see the bomber shortly after it was shot down, as a sort of morale booster.'

'So, you didn't ask your uncle what he was doing there?'

'No, he died before the photo was re-published in a new article in 1960, which an aunt passed on to me.'

'What happened to the crew?'

'I'm not sure, but I will check.'

We started by Blu-tacking the photos to large cardboard sheets, trying to separate them into blocks of mother, father, aunts, and so on. After a couple of 1960hours Vera left me, and then spent almost three-quarters of an hour chatting to Sally. Just what women find to talk about is a mystery. Sally can spend hours on the phone to Jackie and Pam. And, when I ask what they talked about all I got was 'Oh this and that.' On Ladies Day at the golf club, there's a cacophony of noise, everyone talking at once. I'll bet someone has even coined a phrase for that particular noise, a *jabberation of female golfers.*

Chapter 20

Monday 23rd February

The following Monday I attended an appointment with Mr Kassim in the Gardale Radiography Department. He had arranged for me to have an fMRI scan (Functional Magnetic Resonance Imaging). Another consultant would also be attending, a Mr Brian Kettridge, a neurologist and Dr Helen Bolton, a specialist in MRI radiography, because there was general interest in my case.

Before the scan, I told them about my latest flashbacks and how they seemed to coincide with words or ideas particularly associated with strong emotions.

'Does it happen each time you think of something?'

'No, I have tried to induce flashbacks but all I get are memories. For them to occur it seems there has to be a strong element of emotion, fear, or anger. And of course, none of this happened before my accident. There is also a further state.'

'How do you mean?'

'Like nightmares. Black thoughts. An alternate world in which my mother is dead, but I know she's alive. I can normally wake up from these nightmares, but I have been terrified that one time I may not be able to.

'That seems to be bordering on schizophrenia. But I really think, like Mr Kassim, that those black thoughts are due to the trauma of your injury, and I should not concern yourself about them."

Mr Kassim took over. 'Right. We'll conduct the scan now if you feel that you are ready. It's nothing to be worried about and you'll not feel anything unpleasant. Do you think it would be possible for you to try to initiate one of these incidents, or as you describe them, flashbacks, whilst in the machine?' asked Mr Kettridge. 'It might give us a lead as to what's happening inside your brain.'

'Well, I'll try but it doesn't always work.'

As I entered the all enclosing tunnel I didn't have any of the feelings of claustrophobia that terrified some people. I think if you have been potholing and squeezed through impossibly tight passages, and, in water and mud, you're not frightened by a confined space in a machine. But I would have preferred to be inside *and* outside at the same time, actually seeing the results in real time. I relaxed, it was a lot better than being in the dentist's chair, or even the hygienist when she found that sensitive tooth. Nothing seemed to happen for an instant but then, suddenly, *Bang*! I was in our old garage on Stonefield Lane.

'Tommy, for God's sake, will you hold still.'

'Ow can I 'eep still with your vl'oody 'hand in 'me gob?'

'Well if you don't keep still, I can't get this rotten tooth out. It's your choice.'

'Hol' on then' only make it 'whick. Oww! Bloody Hell Ernie, that hurt.'

'Well you said make it quick. And I'm not surprised. Look ... can you see what a monster it was, all decayed. It must have hurt for months. Here, have a drink of water and spit in that bowl.'

'Thanks. Even though it's sore, it feels better already. Nah then, what dust a' owe thee?' Tommy got up and reached for his cap.

'Nothing at the moment but I'll leave that to you to come up with something ... maybe a bit of pork would be nice.'

'There's one of me sows bein' slaughtered next wok. Ah'll mak sure tha gets a slice or two. That okay Ernie?'

'That's great, Tommy . . . then I'll see you in the Cock and Bottle on Sunday. But make sure you keep that gap in your gum clean, and gargle after meals with salt and water.'

And then suddenly "just like that" in Tommy Cooper's words, I was back inside the machine. It was that simple. All I had thought about was dentist, tooth, pain and *bang*. And, there was no feeling of anything bad waiting to happen.

The female radiographer in her trim white uniform with its red flashing extracted me from the humming sarcophagus. Mr Kassim and the others were in a huddle. They were animatedly pointing to something on the computer and beaming, obviously whatever had happened had been successful. After I had dressed, Mr Kassim spoke to me in his consulting room,

'Well, the good news is that there doesn't seem to be any tumour etc and your wound is healing very nicely. But there did seem to be some activity in odd places, which I have not seen before. As you know, there have been huge strides in finding out what goes on in the brain. The fMRI scan allows us to see which parts of your brain are active, for example if I showed you a picture of a girl in a bathing costume it might excite one area connected to sex, another might connect to languages, food and so on. But the area we saw light up was the orbitofrontal cortex, which controls reason and behaviour.

I would like to consult with some of my colleagues and then, if you agree, make some further studies. Would you be agreeable to more tests?' It was obvious that he wanted to continue the investigations.

'Yes, I would like that.' I replied. 'And, can I ask how long I was in the scanner?'.

'About twenty minutes.'

Only it seemed like seconds,'

'I see. ... that's interesting, quite an awareness difference. Another question. Were you aware of anything unusual happening when we artificially excited your amygdala, that's the bit at the back of your head, which controls emotions and so on? For example, did you have any experience, one of your flashbacks?'

'Yes, quite sharp. I was my father taking someone's tooth out.'

'You father? Was he a dentist then.?'

'No, he had trained as a dental mechanic in 1932 but during World War Two he, unofficially, extracted people's teeth and also made them dentures.'

'I see. So, you actually 'saw' him extracting a tooth.'

'Not quite. It appeared that *I* was doing the tooth-pulling. I *was* my father.'

'Can you describe it?'

'Yes, he was pulling a bad tooth from a farmer called Tommy Tompkins. I vaguely remember him. He farms at the top of Broomfield Lane in Higher Wincham – or rather did, he'll be long dead now. He was a miserable old bugger, pardon the French. My father did this work in an old garage in our back garden. Mr Tompkins wasn't the only one. My dad pulled lots of teeth and made umpteen dentures. He had the special rubber powder and equipment which formed the hard dental plates by vulcanisation, and so on'

'You said he wasn't a registered dentist.'

'No, but during the war there were shortages of medical people, dentists and the like, and in any case my dad didn't charge.'

'How do you mean? He didn't get paid for this work?'

'Oh, he got paid all right but in kind. In Tommy Tompkins case it seemed to be a side of pork. Sometimes it was just a pint. There was a lot of bartering in our village.'

'I know exactly what you mean, my father was a doctor in rural Sri Lanka - or Ceylon as it was then - he got a goat once.'

'A goat!'

'Yes, a rather wealthy patient. It symbolised more than payment, it's difficult to explain. But to return to your case. You had an experience and its effect was recorded. We will examine the recording and later you can see for yourself. To help us would you please write down the episode with as much detail as possible'

'So, I'm not going mad.'

'Maybe we are all going mad, but you no more than anyone else.'

Friday 2nd March

Sally thought the whole thing a waste of taxpayer's money, but she was glad that I wasn't going to be packed off to the mental hospital at Menston, at least not yet. Vera found it fascinating and thought perhaps I could use this to find out how my dad got the gun.

'So, the boffins are going to probe your innermost thoughts, are they?' she said in a typical Vera comment.

'I think 'boffins' went out with ground nuts if you remember the waste of money in that Socialist scheme? But to answer your question, they will light up my brain, I will glow in the dark. Actually, I have no idea what will happen, but we shall see. And what have your 'experts' found?'

'It is as I thought, meaningless unless you have a key. There's no cipher pattern, it's a sort of short hand like *t bt p*, which might mean today I bought potatoes but could equally mean Tommy bit Paul. Sorry.'

'At least you tried.'

'Yes, but they will still work on it, maybe some clue will emerge that unlocks the message. There could, however, be consequences relating to that piece of polythene with the microdots if we pursue it. It's more complicated because it is stolen property.'

'How do you mean?'

'Well, the microdots appear to give exact details of the process at the time and drawings of the equipment etc. This technically belongs to the company. That means ICI.'

'What are you saying? That my father stole it?'

'Well, you found it in his things, so, presumably, it was your father who took it.'

'Now I was getting annoyed. All I was trying to find out was the truth of what happened and once again you, or the people you know, are suggesting a crime.'

'I'm not saying that there will be any problem but if we take it further, are you prepared for what might happen?'

'If it solves the mystery and helps us to find out why my dad had it – and, of course, the gun – then yes.'

'That's fine then, I will take it and the photographs you made and see if 'they' can be persuaded to pursue what is actually on the dots and their meaning. They have the equipment to examine them in far greater detail. But it may take time.'

'That's no problem and, once again, thanks. How do you do it?'

'What?'

'I mean you must have very good friends to be able to enlist their help after all this time. I mean … with you having retired and all that.'

'Don't ask, and I'll tell you no lies, *"There are more things twixt heaven and earth than are dreamt of, Horatio."'*

'Huh?'

'Let's just say some links are never broken. Okay.'

'Right. *Then into your hands I commend my notes.*' I thought I'd try my best to counter her quotation, but it didn't seem to have the same ring.

'Have you tried looking at the documents and photos to see whether they trigger any memory?'

'Yes, I have tried and tried but nothing will come. Of course, some jog my memory of a house or, for example, Sheba, the cocker spaniel dog belonging to my grandmother but nothing to trigger any flashbacks There was nothing either in the boxes that suggested a link. It seems to come when you least expect it. but that MRI machine seemed to make it easier for some reason.'

'Are you sure that we have everything? I mean every book or notebook?'

'I'll ask my mother whether she has anything, but we did sort things out before she moved house. It's worth asking, however. It just so happens that we'll be going over to see her next week. I can ask then.'

Chapter 21

Cobble Cottage in Robin Hoods Bay was situated on the left-hand side towards the bottom of New Road, the steepest road in England except for some in Cornwall. There was no parking adjacent to it, so we had to use the Scarborough Borough Council park at the top of the hill and walk down. That's easy, it's the walk back that's a killer.

Its front bay window had an uninterrupted view of the grey Redcar mudstone on the beach with its fossils. There are ammonites to be found on the north side by the cliffs, but it is much too dangerous, there, for children, due to possible rockfalls. Even in fairly recent times, the cobles would be pulled up out of the sea's reach and the locals would buy their fish direct, without the need for any fishmonger. All changed now; the cobles have gone: where there had been fish, now the odd boat netted tourists.

It was still a lovely place and the pub at the bottom, the Bay Hotel, was a favourite of mine. Aptly named because of its location next to the sea, but also because of its bay windows, which jutted out allowing a great view. When young, Jackie and Pamela loved digging in the dark sand for treasure buried by the pirates. Of course, Robin Hoods Bay had changed, and in my opinion not for the better. Whereas the old shops had supplied the needs of the locals, now they were boutiques and studios selling kitsch to the tourists.

Sally normally came with me but on this occasion had another commitment, so I was by myself. I walked down to the beach and stood perched on one of the rocky slabs on the shore. The climate was normally bracing and today, within seconds, the wind whipped away any remnant of sleep. In the winter, this wind would strip your bones clean within minutes, even now in February it went straight through my anorak and I hurried back for my breakfast, bacon and two eggs, my dad's favourite and his downfall.

'Mum, did we miss anything when we moved you? You remember, we went through Dad's things and I took most things to Birchcroft. But was there anything of Dad's that might have been forgotten?'

'What did you do with his truss?'

'His truss!' I said. 'Oh Lord, I hadn't thought about that for years.

'You know he had a rupture and he had that thing made from lead and leather, to keep the muscle in place and stop it hurting. Where did it go? Did Tom have it?'

I knew that truss well because when he dropped it on the wooden floor it sounded like a cannon going off.

'Mum I've no idea, probably, the tip. I don't expect the church would have taken it. '

'Oh, of course they would, they might have wanted it for Africa. You know, that's where all the old false teeth go - and spectacles.' I sighed because I'd heard the story many times before. Mum had been in the hospital at Middlesbrough and had had a colostomy. When she was wheeled back to the ward, the nurses had forgotten to send her teeth back with her. She started telling them forcibly and loudly not to send them to Africa as she needed them herself. I remember the nurses doubling up with laughter, at the same time assuring her that they were safe. Then she told us that it was all right 'they were in transit'. This became a tale told at all the reunions including wakes.

'Never mind the truss Mum. Were there any books?'

'Yes, there were lots from ICI.'

'Were they from Winnington, or from Wilton?'

'Oh, mainly from Wilton I think. Winnington was a long time ago you know. In any case, *you* took them.'

'Yes, I know it was a long time ago. Would you show me what you still have here?'

On her bookcase were four bibles (because we kept buying them for birthday presents with larger print each time as her eyesight deteriorated); books about Royal Family, Mother Teresa, French Impressionists (when she was in the art mode) the Tudors (when she was in the history mode) and local books on Whitby (when she was with the jet-set!) and various visits by the Alpha Group to old churches.

There was also an old Walker family bible, the sort started in Victorian times and kept up to date for several decades. In it were the sepia coloured photos of our ancestors, a lot of them unidentifiable, the women in dark heavy looking dresses and the men in stand-up collars and huge mutton-chop beards.

There was a box built into the back in which trinkets and knick-knacks could be stored. Lockets containing hair, a Whitby jet brooch (souvenir of outings) and so on.

I sat down in the armchair nearest to the electric fire and fumbled through the contents, taking each one out and laying it on the table in the kitchen, and found at the bottom a heavily Sellotaped packaged bundle. I knew this had been wrapped by my father, it was his trademark. Bless him. Then, despite being warm a minute ago I was suddenly freezing.

1953 a few days before Christmas

My satchel was full of Christmas cards and it was heavy and wet. My thoughts were on the warmth inside our house and some hot grub. It was the end of term time and, in order to earn some cash, I, and a few others had signed up as temporary postmen to ease the seasonal burden on the regulars.

One of the problems was that I thought that I knew Wincham quite well but, obviously, there were tiny back streets that were unknown to me by name. I had been down them many times but never bothered to look at their names. In the worst cases, there weren't any names. Everybody who lived there knew them, but I didn't. I knew *Broadway*, which had nothing to do with Hollywood; *Shoots Lane,* so-called because it was next to the woods where the men shot the rooks every Spring; *Gunners Clough*, where there'd been a battle during the Civil War, *New Street,* full of old terraced houses from the 19th century, and others, like *Lovers Lane* and so on which must have been popular way back. Sometimes the numbers just stopped only to reappear on a completely unconnected street. For the first couple of days I floundered and had to stop people and ask. How many were wrongly delivered I don't know. I was probably saved only because it was Christmas and people were in a generous mood.

The temperature had dropped sharply, and sleet was falling. Not crisp snow but freezing sleet, half-rain half-ice. At the end of the afternoon I had one package left but had no idea who it was for. It was dark, and I couldn't decipher the address. The devil in me said throw it away or take it back and admit your failure. Both ideas were being considered.

'Oh, Lord, did I really drop it into someone else's box?' I murmured out loud.

'Why would you do that?' my mother said, 'I came to ask if you wanted a cup of tea? And what's that?' she said tapping the little package.

'Eh? Oh, sorry I must have been dreaming… er … I found this in the old family bible. Do you know what it is?'

'Never seen it before. What's in it?'

'Shall I open it?'

'Why not.'

Examining the package, which was about three inches wide and four long, I saw that I couldn't possibly peel off all the Sellotape and would have to use a sharp knife or scissors to cut it.

'Have you got a sharp, pointed knife?' I asked my mother.

'Yes, I'll go and fetch one.'

The outside had originally been of brown paper but was now hard and rigid, because of the Sellotape in which it had been smothered. When she returned I used the point of the knife to carefully cut through three edges until I could peel back the top. Inside was a small notebook.

'Let me see,' said my mother, holding it up to the light streaming in through the window, and opening the first page.

'It's gibberish, all numbers, and dates and designs.'

'Can I take a look?' I asked.

It was obvious to me that it wasn't meant to be read easily. There had to be some message in it, but it would take somebody better than me with puzzles to figure it out. Fortunately, I thought, I know someone who could!

'I'll have to take it with me, Mother, and see what I can make of it. Will that be okay? Oh, and do you have such a thing as a rubber band?'

'I save rubber bands, you know, they always come in useful,' she said returning and handing me a red one. 'That one came from the bank,' she said. I closed the top back like a clam shell and put the rubber band round it to keep it intact.

As I motored back to Grisedale, I wondered what had I done with that other package so long ago? Had I really pushed it through the nearest letterbox?

Friday 7th March

'What do you make of it?' I asked Vera. 'Of course, it might mean nothing. It might just be useless jottings, and my mother suggested it might have something to do with the football pools. My dad and my grandfather used to do them every week without fail.'

We were having a specially convened meeting to discuss the new find.

'I'll probably need help myself. You realise I'm not eighteen any longer; at least half of my brain cells have more than likely disappeared.'

'Was that how old you were when you were at Bletchley?'

'No, I was actually nineteen when I started there; it was 1943 and I had just finished my first year at Oxford. I had to complete my degree later after the war'

'So, they yanked you out of Uni'?'

'Yes, fairly shortly after I did that crossword published in the *Daily Telegraph*, my tutor came to see me to explain that it was in the national interest for me to leave university and join a special group at Bletchley Park.'

'*My* tutor said I had to work harder to get any sort of degree at all,' I said with a pout.

'You've done all right though, haven't you?'

'I suppose so. But I always wanted to do more research, but you know…'

'And then there was Sally?'

'Yes, and it turned out to be the best damned thing I ever did…but don't you tell her that.' She laughed,

'I promise … as long as you stop swearing.'

'*God Dammit, Blast and Bloody Hell.* There, that's it, all finished,' I said. She just shook her head,

'Impossible. You've a rebellious streak in you, you know. Anyway, let's see what we have.'

I glanced at the first line:

S 62 su ba be ad. da -Q —+ v22 n M6-2bf ae.df αβ+Q O ÷≤β x ct W " " Ø

The pages were full of this sort of stuff.

My brain had baulked quite quickly at this mass of symbols, when I had first seen them. My mother said he was good at drawing trees but not much else. Vera was fascinated.

'Clearly there are patterns but, of course, it is possible that it is a one-off cypher, which may be insoluble like the other one. The first few pages seem to be composed of symbols and odd letters sprinkled in amongst them; the pages later on appear to be normal script, but in code form. In a way it looks like a diary. Can I take it, I promise to return it either way?'

'Yes, that will be fine, but should we make a photocopy - just in case it disappears like the gun!' I said.

'I agree, it's a good idea in any case. Let's make three copies of each page… but I promise you this will not be impounded.'

Chapter 22

A letter arrived inviting me to attend a meeting at the Faculty of Biological Sciences, Leeds University to discuss possible trials connected with what had happened in the fMRI scan.

'What we would like to do is to run tests using a slightly different MRI scanner, a Tesla MRI, it's much more powerful. Then, we would like to try to repeat the experience that you had the last time, or similar, and to correlate it with episodes that you have had previously...' Sally was horrified when I told her,

'They're going to use you as a guinea pig and mess about with your mind.'

'Yes, but if it stops those dizzy moments surely that's a good thing?'

'But they might make it worse. How do you know what might happen?' What Sally didn't know was that I had another agenda. I wanted to be able to control what happened and direct where my flashback took me. I had a feeling that their experiments might just help me to do this. I was still fascinated by the possibility of being able to put the clock back. If my mother could speak to me in her dream why could I not warn my mother to avoid that grate.

As Sally was burbling away, I was pondering just how different my brain was to hers, even before the accident. Why was my brain programmed *t'other* way round? It was quite common in the past, particularly in the rural areas if you were born *cack-handed*, to have your left hand tied behind your back. I have read that this sometimes resulted in the development of a stammer. In my case, perhaps combined with jaundice at birth, the result was total. No stammer, but all the functions, normally residing in my right side, were transferred to the left.

At football, as in most sports, initially, there were advantages; my left cross was wicked, but my right one tended to go in exactly the same direction. The Sport's Master, Mr. Evans, because I was a small lad, wanted me to bowl slow left-arm leg breaks; I wanted to bowl fast. I was banned from hockey for ever, because the sports mistress wouldn't let me turn my stick over! I boxed, and my nose assumed a position semi-permanently to the left. I took up fencing in Canada and it was necessary to buy a special left-handed foil blade from somewhere deep in the middle of the USA, costing three times as much as the normal right-handed one!

During basic training in the RAF, the drill sergeant said that I would chop my thumb off, if I tried to reload the 303 Enfield with my left hand - the bolt being on the right-hand side, convenient for right handers. I replied that I preferred to live with no thumb than die *intactus* because I couldn't hit a barn door shooting right handed. My musing stopped as I realised that Sally was still talking,

'By the way, I told Ian that you had had more than enough eggs.'

'Good I was getting egg-bound and starting to cluck every time the cock crowed.'

Left to myself I thought some more about my dad and his work in the Polythene Plant at Wallerscote. He died in 1968 just hours before he was due to go into work at Wilton - still making polythene. He and uncle Bill spent most of their working lives producing polythene, originally called *Alkathene*, ICI's trade mark. They experienced the transition from a secret project during the war to the acceptance of the material as a 'work horse' plastic, particularly in the later versions. At the present time, it enjoys a secure place as the most popular material for many items, such as food storage boxes and the ubiquitous polythene bags, being none toxic.

Unfortunately, its very properties and its misuse by humans have now caused it to be an environmental nightmare.

The reason for the location of the original Brunner Mond plant at Winnington, was the proximity of the River Weaver which was navigable and enabled ships from Brunner Mond, later becoming ICI or Imperial Chemical Industries, to reach the North Sea and to connect with the Manchester Ship Canal. There was also a useful connection to the Mersey and Trent canal by the Anderton boat Lift that I had mentioned before. In the early days the traffic was in salt and soda ash, or caustic soda. My Uncle Harold, husband to Aunt Lily, was captain of one of these ships.

'Right, first of all we will put this gel on your head, then we attach these wires…don't worry there will not be any shocks.'

'How do you know? I might shock you, by starting to swear or something.'

'No, it doesn't work like that. What results there are, if any, will be shown on our computers. But you have a button in each hand Press the left one if you experience anything and the right one if you have any pain or you wish us to stop. Okay?' The technicians fussed with some things, but I told myself *that's over my head*. I laughed at my own joke. The clinician looked surprised.

'Did you experience something already? But we haven't started yet.'

'No, I'm sorry I just thought of something funny.'

Mr Kassim looked at his colleagues and looked at the ceiling as if to say I hope that we're not wasting our time with this one.

'Now we will start by stimulating different parts of your cortex. All you have to do is let us know if anything happens. Remember the left button for an experience and the right one for pain.'

I felt a warm sensation as though I had entered a sauna. It was really very pleasant.

It's very early in the morning and, today, it's my job to empty the eel pots. Opposite the church I turn through the gate and walk down the field to the mere. I'm glad of my wellies as the dew is heavy on the long grass. It's late autumn, 1918, and everyone's glad that the war has finished but it doesn't seem to make any difference to me. I still have to do my jobs, war or peacetime.

I know it has to be done, but why couldn't my mum have more boys, then it could be shared. Mrs Jones has seven kids, including four boys. It's not fair.

Ugh... this water's freezing ... anyway, let's see what we've got. Pulling up the eel-pot, marked Foster, I counted as best as I could; there were several all twisted up together in a writhing knot. Putting on my thick gloves, I grasp the head of one of the wriggling eels and hit the back of its head with the paternoster. I dropped it into the wicker basket and then dealt with the next one and so on until the pot was empty. Seven, I counted, not bad. Mum will be happy. Now back for some breakfast ...

'How was that, Robert? Did you experience anything?'

'Yes, it was fantastic because I went back, either as a memory of what I've been told, but which was buried in my subconscious, or, believing to be my father, experiencing something before I was born.'

'You told me that in an earlier flashback...let us call it that ... your mother spoke to you when she was a young girl and, obviously, before you were born.'

'Yes, that's correct, and my mother has no recollection of telling me.'

'So, could it be ...and we are only surmising ... that her memory was somehow implanted in you, at birth."

'Ye-es, but she told me that I was in *her* dream. And are you saying that my dad somehow gave me a memory of himself as a youngster?'

'I don't know what to think. It could be, of course, that you are making it up,' but he added quickly, 'subconsciously, or hallucinating due to your head injury, which is another way of saying the same thing. Let me say straight away, that I don't believe that you're faking these, *whatever*, they are. It's all very interesting. We'll examine the data recorded during that latest incident and will come back to you.

And just to give you a little more background, what we are doing is using the fMRI scan to see what we call haemodynamic responses when you have your visions. That's just a fancy term for the patterns of blood flow in your brain. Are you interested?'

'Definitely. Yes please … please do carry on. Obviously, I've a strong personal reason to know what's happening in my brain. Anything which would make sense of the … whatever.'

'There are an increasing number of studies along the same lines. One was by two Finns, Jääskeläinen and Pajula, a Chinese neurologist, and others whose names I forget, in which they showed patients comedy clips and observed the activity in the right frontal lobe and in other cortical areas. So, what we are doing is the same sort of thing but in reverse. You are providing the activity with your visions, we just give you a little nudge as it were. Okay?'

'Yes, that's fine and thank you for the explanation and your interest.' I can tell you that I quite enjoyed the experience, which was not accompanied by any dizziness or anxiety.'

'You're saying that the feeling was different to those which occurred as it were naturally.'

'Yes. In some I felt sick … er nauseous.'

'That *is* interesting.'

On returning home it seemed that whatever the scientists had done had increased my mind's activity. I was experiencing more and more of my mother and father's early lives. As soon as I slept, or even snoozed I would see them, or be them.

I liked the idea put forward by Mr Kassim that they could be implanted memories but reminded myself that my mother had "spoken" to me. In one sense I was more relaxed because there were experts who were believing what I was saying and putting forward ideas; again, it was a load shared. I thought I should tell Vera. I just told Sally that tests were being carried out and that I had nothing seriously wrong with me.

That night I just slipped into one of the most complete and satisfying dreams since my accident. Clearly that test at Leeds had opened something up and, also, I felt that I was on the right track to make some discovery about my mother, or my father that was important. Now that I had help from Vera I felt so much more relaxed.

. Just before I went to bed I dug out my birth certificate dated Twenty-second of April 1933, noting, as I knew, that the occupation of the father was 'Navvy'.

Chapter 23

1933

'I know it's not much of a job digging ditches but it's the best I can do at the moment,' said Bert, the husband of Jinny who was the half-sister of Alice, my wife.

Bert was a foreman in the High Leigh Council's Building and Works department and had managed to get me a job as a navvy. I knew that my father, William, was outraged at me taking it, but I had to have a job: I needed the money. Alice was pregnant and the apprenticeship as Dental Mechanic had finished. The dentist had apologised and given me a very good reference, saying that he just couldn't afford to keep me on. I knew that this wasn't the whole truth, he could get another apprentice easily enough, probably, at a lower wage There were just too many people out of work.

'No problem Bert, it'll bring in some money until I find something else …and thanks, we are both very grateful.'

'When's Alice due, by the way,' Bert asked, 'Jinny said it was soon?'

'In about six weeks they say. There's a resident nurse in the hall and she has been very good in helping Alice over her sickness.'

'Is it a boy or a girl? Of course, you won't know but what's your bet?' I just shrugged my shoulders and laughed.

It was hard work, but it was a good Spring and little rain. Being as most of the work was centred around High Leigh, it was close to Ditton where Alice and I had rented a small cottage on the Ditton Estate belonging to Lord Horeshom. It was an easy bike ride home. The men, I was working with were a bit cautious, because they knew Bert was some relation and also because I told them that I had gone to Winsford Grammar. But a few pints at the Black Bull soon melted the ice. One lad couldn't read, and I tried to teach him in any spare time we had. It made me realise how lucky I was that my mother and father had paid for my education. My father was a foreman mechanic at Brunner Mond Winnington. He was trying to find me a place there for me.

1934

'There's a new plant starting up at Wallerscote in 1935 making a new material,' said my dad William. 'Some sort of Bakelite manufacture, but that's all I know. I've managed to get you an interview and told them that you had experience of mouldings and vulcanising rubber. It's next Monday, 9 o'clock, with a Dr Freeth.'

'So, Mr Foster, I understand that you were a Dental Mechanic. Why did you give that profession up?'

'I didn't give it up, it was just that there were no vacancies. All the dentists, I contacted, already had staff and my wife was expecting a baby. I had to support her. A relation got me a temporary job with the local council.' He nodded.

'I understand that you are familiar with rubber and have used high pressure in making dental plates for false teeth?'

'Yes, that's by the vulcanisation of rubber in autoclaves, basically heat and pressure. I'm also familiar with casting gold for implants and so on.'

'Right. You had a Grammar school education it says.'

'Yes, at Winsford Grammar for boys, initially as a border.'

'And which subjects did you take?'

'The normal; Latin, French, History, Geography, Chemistry and Mathematics. Oh, and I played a violin in the school orchestra and played once with Yehudi Menuhin when he paid a visit to the school.

'Good … good. Then all that seems satisfactory. I understand that your father is a foreman mechanic in the soda ash plant. Would that be William Foster?'

'Yes, he told me about the position that was coming up.'

'He was a good sprinter you know. Raced several times for Brunner Mond. Anyway, thank you for coming, we will write to you. It would, initially, be a labourer's job but with good prospects for chargehand. I cannot tell you many more details at this stage, but the process will be to make a new type of plastic.'

Chapter 24

This new treatment with Mr Kassim and Dr Noble was great because it got rid of the 'black' thoughts, and that dreadful slide into a sort of brown no man's land, where it had been impossible to choose where I went. I suppose that by energising certain parts of my brain, they were assisting the healing process, but they had done something else as well.

I could dream, *or invent*, my father's history without that dizzy feeling. The doctors had done something to my brain, which allowed me, more easily, to imagine or relive things I had known or heard about my dad, even those that were buried in my subconscious, without feeling sick. I tried a little experiment which was to think of the one great thing that my dad and I did together. Fishing.

Just by the top of the Anderton Boat Lift are several reservoirs. They had been built as emergency reserves of drinking water, but as far as we were concerned, they were for us as youngsters to play in and around, and in particular to fish in. All three were the hallowed preserve of the Anderton Angling Society 'membership by invitation only!'.

Within the club, there was an even more prestigious section, named the '30 Club'. As is indicated by its name, membership of it was restricted to 30 anglers. My Uncle Albert was a star member; sometimes Secretary, sometimes President, and often took the major prizes. My Father, Uncle Eddie and later, on his return from the war, Uncle Ron, were all members of this inner sanctum.

Members of the Anderton Angling Society were allowed to fish in reservoirs numbers 2 and 3, one of which was used for stocking purposes. Reservoir 1 was reserved for competitions and used solely by members of the '30 club'.

In order to describe 'fishing', I must leap about in time because events took place over many years and it is impossible to keep a strict chronology. Fishing was not a sport, it was a way of life, it was breathed, it was dreamed about; plots were made to seize committee positions, and schemes were hatched to win prizes. There were also conspiracies, cliques, conniving and straight forward, down and out cheating! Special oils, involving pheromones, were sought to increase the attractiveness of the bait. fishing was also very special to me, because of the time I spent with my father.

Because I had been fishing since six or seven and had had to use whatever tackle was available, initially, bamboo canes, cotton lines, bent pins and home-made floats, once I got into the real stuff, meaning greenheart three-piece rods and tinted nylon lines on reels, it was easy. When I was eleven, I went with my dad to a competition, on No. 1 Court! This particular morning my uncles were away because of holidays, and there were vacant spaces, so my dad enquired if I could join in. Since I was clearly no threat, I was duly entered, and my dad paid the entry fee of one shilling for me. Places were allocated by drawing numbered discs from a bag; these corresponded to places around the reservoir. It was known which positions fished better than others, but no one really bothered when I was allocated number one, which was a very good spot. Being young, I was very quick, and the technique gained early, meant that very soon I had a keepnet full of fish, all small. At the weigh-in my total was easily the best; thus, I had won the kitty- probably eighteen or nineteen shillings.

At this point, the rule book was hastily produced by the runner up, and there was an emergency committee meeting, which decided that a certain age had to be attained before you were eligible to compete. I was, therefore, disqualified and stripped of my victory; my dad had his shilling ritually returned. It wasn't 'thirty pieces of silver' but it felt like it.

The season ended in December and prizes were awarded at the Annual Dinner, for the best score amassed during the twelve months' weekly competitions. The points for each competition were; three for a first place, two for second, and one for the third. For the year in question, my Uncle Albert was in line to win the first prize, but he had a rival, Bernard Hobbs, who was two points ahead. If Uncle Albert came first with Bert second, Albert lost. If Albert came first and Bert third, it was a tie, BUT, here the tie breaker came in. In the event of a tie, the person who had caught the heaviest single fish, during the season, won. That person in the previous matches had been Bernard.

There was an extraordinary meeting of the 'war cabinet', three uncles and dad. It was agreed that if any of the three, not in line for the annual prize, drew a place near to the rival, they were to ensure his failure, that is they would 'nobble' him!

My father was never especially worried whether he won or lost. He was, in this respect a disappointment to the others. He just liked fishing, however, he would out of loyalty play his part, if required. It was therefore the cruel hand of fate that decided he would be *the* one, the 'nobbler'.

Prepared, just in case, he took with him bread paste laced with the household bleach, *Domestos*. Once again fate intervened, and he was drawn next to Bernard. My dad did his best and proceeded, legally, to throw large handfuls of ground bait but, illegally, it was laced with the bleach and landed too close to Bernard's float. My dad apologised, of course, for his carelessness! He then baited his hook with the bleach-rich paste.

When Bernard started to catch fish, in telephone numbers, my dad received glares and desperate signals were given by my Uncle Albert to step up the interference. Unbelievably, my dad then started to catch dozens of fish *himself*, on this most unpleasant bait; my Uncle Albert was apoplectic!

At the weigh-in my Dad came second; Uncle Albert was third; Bernard took first place and won the annual prize by four points. I cannot describe but I heard about the subsequent shouting match between my Dad and Uncle Albert. Years later at family gatherings, this too became a huge joke and trotted out as the best laid plans ganging *oft' afgley*.

I remembered another fishing trip, one that was earlier, and I was by myself. It was special for a particular reason. This time, using my new ability I deliberately went back to that day.

It was a glorious September day, 1941, and warm, with just the odd cloud floating above. I had decided this particular day was a fishing day.

One of my favourite pastimes was fishing for small carp. It was fun anyway to pull out the small golden wriggling fish on the end of my line, and pop it into my bucket, but there was an extra purpose because my uncles gave me one penny for each. That was the deal: one penny for one small golden carp. Uncle Albert kept them in an old bathtub ready for use as live-bait to catch jack pike, which was pretty good to eat.

I set off with the normal warnings from my mother,

'…Don't go too near the edge and fall in … and don't fish where there's jinny green teeth … and don't go and tear your pullover on barbed wire, or there'll be trouble; I'm sick and tired of mending tears.'

'Yes Mum … no Mum.' I replied with a secret smile knowing that I was going to break most of the rules. What I didn't know was this was when her back problems were starting. Had I been giving any thought to anything other than going fishing, I would have seen that she was looking pale and drawn.

It was about a mile and a half over the *Brooms,* a gentle hill, then past *Lovers Lane*. Even though I knew there wouldn't be any courting couples along it at this time of the day, I couldn't resist a look - just to check. At the end of the track, I climbed over the stile and crossed the road, which led to Taylor's Hollow, then over another stile and through the wood to the three clay pits. I had been told by my Grandpa Walker that they had once been used to store and mature slaked lime, which was used as a building material superior to mortar.

The three were now joined together like a cloverleaf surrounded by hazel bushes. It was a place of silence and mystery. The largest pond was where I would fish for the golden carp; the smallest was too shallow for fish and more of a marsh. The middle pond was full of male newts or, as we called them, askers. These were terrible, all orange and red squirming and wriggling. The only way to get rid of them off your line was to cut it, which meant rigging up with another bent pin.

My bait was soft white bread mixed with a little milk and kneaded with a knife or in the hand, until it made a soft-ish paste. Not too soft, or it would simply fall off. Also, the carp loved to suck at the bait rather than bite it, so you had to make it hard enough to make them impatient.

Around part of the pond where I fished were bulrushes, which stood tall and erect like grenadier guards. My Grandma Walker had them painted with gold paint then stuck them in a vase as a decoration. I got into trouble for picking at them to expose the soft velvety seeds. Unfortunately, you couldn't push them back.

As always, I marvelled at the smell of the pond. It was an intense rich smell of decaying weeds mixed with the earthy smell of black ooze. It seemed absolutely right for a pond to smell this way. If you pushed a stick into the ooze and then retrieved it, the stick would be covered with black mud and full of wriggling, slimy creatures.

My fishing gear was a cane specially chosen by my Grandpa Walker. He knew what was required, what it had to do; long enough but not too long. My line was sewing cotton or, sometimes, the thicker thread used for securing buttons. My hook was a pin, sharpened a little at its point and bent just so, with the help of my dad's pliers – I like to think they were the ones he used to pull out teeth, but that's another story. My float was a suitably stripped hen's wing feather and held to the line with a piece of bicycle rubber valve. The split lead weights were 'borrowed' from my Dad's fishing tackle. I could have used an actual fish hook, but this was not as good because it took longer to get the fish off, particularly, if it had swallowed the hook, then you needed a paternoster to disgorge it.

Part of the enjoyment was to cast the line with its little blob of bait on the end into the pond and watch it slowly sink until the float stood upright. Ripples spread out from the float in perfect symmetry across the water until they died out. Because today was without wind, the surface became like glass and so transparent that I had to keep my shadow well away, otherwise the fish would be frightened off. I waited. Sometimes, you would have to wait patiently for a considerable time. Today I was lucky, after a few minutes I saw the tiniest of bob of the float with a minute circular ripple. This was judgement time. Wait. If I struck too early the line would come up with an empty hook as the sudden jerk tore off the bait and I would have to start all over again. Wait. Now the bobbing became more insistent.

Then the float jerked downwards just by a fraction. I struck and lifted up the end of the rod. On the hook was a frantically wriggling fish, gleaming gold in the sunlight. I swung the line over the bucket filled with pond water and shook off the fish. I re-baited my hook and repeated the process until I had eleven. One more would mean twelve pennies, which would buy two comics form the paper shop.

In went my bait. There was a sudden swirl in the water and, when I struck, I realised that I had something much heavier on the end. I managed to guide it to the bank and lifted it out. Instead of a tiddler I had caught a monster. It was so big that its tail stuck out of the top of the bucket and I raced home to tell my dad. It was the biggest fish that I had ever caught.

'So, what are you going to do with it?' he asked, not impressed. 'Are you going to eat it?'

I said, 'No, I don't think carp are good to eat, are they?'

'The monks ate them, they kept carp ponds. Well then, what are you going to do? It's too big to keep, it will die.'

'What should I do then?' I asked.

'Take it back to where you caught it.'

I pondered about that and noticed that my Dad seemed worried about something, preoccupied.

Obviously, I had to take it back, but I wanted to keep it for a bit longer, and it would take me over an hour to go to the pond and back. I decided to keep it overnight and take it back the next day.

We had a small zinc bath that we used for chicken feed and that was big enough. The problem was that the amount of the pond water in the bucket wouldn't be enough to keep the fish alive. We had a tub of rainwater but how to transfer the water from it into the bath? I could have used a jug but that seemed long winded.

This was the day when I discovered what a siphon was. I found a piece of rubber tubing and leaving one end in the tub sucked to bring some water through. It tasted horrible and I spat it out but when I put the tube into the bath I was amazed because the water kept flowing. Why? I watched in amazement as the water transferred itself until there was more than enough. Then after tipping the carp into the bath I ran inside to tell my dad that I had discovered something miraculous. His answer, which seemed uncharacteristically brusque was,

'It's not a new discovery, it's called a siphon.'

I came back to the present feeling quite sad. I remember that I had been elated at my 'discovery' and felt that my Dad's reaction was like a douche of cold water; he could have let me down more lightly. I wish now that I had had the chance of asking him whether I had caught him at the wrong moment, or whether I'd been over excited, and it was his way of bringing me down to reality. Then a sudden thought struck me. That was about the time when my mother was becoming sick. It was possible that I had the answer. He was worried. How time could alter one's perceptions. I thought to check.

Thinking of altered perception, I remembered that I had actually written down an account of one fishing project when I was eighteen. It was in the summertime after finishing school, and before starting at the Tech. After reading Isaac Walton's Compleat Angler I decided to follow his as-it-were recipes to catch particular fish.

I dug about in the box labelled 'Old Misc.' On the top were some old exam papers and just to look at them scared me silly, never mind being able to provide answers. I read something, somewhere, about brain cells deteriorating after twenty at a prodigious rate!

There were some old menus, including one from my graduation dinner, about which the only thing I recall as memorable, was that before the meal one chap keeled over backwards. Bang. Out cold. "Drugs" someone said, but I have no recollection whatsoever what happened to him. All of these were put to one side to go back into the box with their memories, probably only to be discarded by my children after my decease.

Then, success. There it was. I read through the yellowing pages:

My weekends were often taken up with trips to Marbury Mere, a wonderful stretch of water, elliptical in shape, situated close to Great

Budworth and perhaps thirty to forty minutes from Wincham by bicycle. The mere was surrounded with reeds complete with reed warblers, bulrushes, water lilies, swans, moorhens, and coots. In it were bream, roach, dace, perch and the granddaddy of them all, jack pike (Esox Lucius).

My uncles had a boat and in it you could get out those extra twenty or so feet to where the fish were. Whilst I had fished on and off for a large part of my life, there was a period when nothing else seemed to matter. The goal was to succeed; to catch that one fish, which no one else had ever seen - naturally it had also to be a monster - the biggest of its kind.

Isaak Walton in 1653 wrote 'the Compleat Angler'; which whilst being a piece of classic literature, is also a descriptive masterpiece of its subject, notably that Angling is an art. In 1951, nearly three hundred years later, I read it over and over again, imbibing the richness, literally drooling at the texture of his word pictures, his capturing of that one moment in time, for ever and the simple clarity of his recipes or instructions, which I intended to follow to the letter.

An example in Chapter five is where Piscator talks to his companion Venator about baits and discusses worms and giving examples of some types:

"earth-worm; the dug-worm; maggot or gentle; dew-worm; or lob-worm, some of which are called squirrel tails; brandling; marsh-worm; the tag-tail; flag- worm; the dock-worm; the oak-worm; the gilt-tail; the twachel"; and many others too numerous to name.

Each one is then discussed, with the best methods of keeping them in perfect health, so that they are more effective when used. In the case of the brandling, he devotes half a page advising how, if they are sick, "to feed them with beaten up egg and cream so that they will recover"! He also advises the use of "camphire" to add flavour to your worms and gives them a strong and "so tempting a smell, that fish fare the worse and you the better". My uncles didn't think of this.

Firstly, I had to choose the target of my devotions; I chose the Bronze Bream (Abramis brama). This fish can reach seventeen pounds in weight although seven is more likely.

When it takes the bait, the bite is so typical that you know, immediately, exactly what it is. The float rises up in the water, straight up, and lies flat on the surface for a moment; then down it goes into the depths, with the line screaming on the reel. By this time your heart is pounding, you can feel the weight of the fish. It was the obvious choice.

For this fish, Walton had a complete prescription, including what you needed to do at "eight or nine of the clock in the evening", the night prior to actually fishing:

"You shall take a peck or a peck and a half of sweet gross-ground barley-malt; and boil it in a kettle, one or two warms is enough: then strain it through a bag into a tub, the liquor whereof hath done my horse much good".

At this point, I reluctantly had to admit partial defeat. We didn't have barley malt, so I used barley grains. Also, by this time we no longer had chickens and therefore could not even give it to them, thus, not wishing to drink it myself, had to pour this, obviously beneficial liquor, down the drain. The barley grains were for ground bait and, I had to cycle at dusk to Marbury and throw handfuls of the stuff into the mere. Not in any old place, but according to Isaac, precisely where it "was observed the rays of the rising sun, first struck the surface of the water".

The beautiful language and sense of it all was catching so, six days I *thither went, in rain and shine* with the ground-bait. On the seventh, I arranged to borrow the boat and with flasks of hot tea and sandwiches – plus, of course, the special bait, - set off before dusk and rowed out to the chosen spot. It was essential to be in position before dark, so that you were ready at the point of sunrise.

To keep warm, I had on my Harris Tweed jacket, several sweaters, and a woollen Donkey Jacket. To sleep on, I had, of course, several large polythene sacks which had contained animal feed.

Sleep wouldn't come but this was of no great matter, because these are the moments when there can be great reflection. Perhaps I wondered whether Isaac had, actually, ever carried out what he wrote and proposed, or whether it was just surmise.

At two o'clock the clouds rolled back, and the sky became clear. There was a moon, almost full and I can imagine little more wonderful than to lie still and warm, in a small boat looking at the lake in all its serenity with hardly a ripple. The boat was a little out from the reeds in a clear patch, surrounded by water lilies.

The night itself is never absolutely quiet and suddenly a flock of starlings erupted into chatter. My sense of wonder was interrupted by a sudden thought, a question, the answer to which, I had no way of obtaining from Walton. If the birds perceived that the moon equated to light, and therefore sunrise, would the bream come to the same conclusion? Great doubts came into my mind and the thought of wasting a week of preparation, just to let the moment go, without making a move was too much. Grumbling and swearing not a little, I baited up with the brandlings and cast in on both sides of the boat - being greedy, and wanting to double the chances, but, again as recommended by the master. Almost as soon as the baits dropped down to the bottom, the fish struck. Both rods bent almost double and the lines raced underneath the boat, then snapped. It was as though submarines had snagged the hooks and with complete indifference feeling their resistance merely as spider's threads, had proceeded on their way. It all happened in a second, and I was left numb, looking at my useless tackle. The moon then disappeared under clouds and there was nothing more to do except to wait for the dawn, feeling thoroughly miserable.

The sun didn't arrive as a bright corona, a dazzling orb in an azure sky. It 'snook' in with hardly any change whatsoever; the black became dark grey, then the dark grey lightened until the murk was fully lit. Drizzle followed and despite re-tackling and staying until twelve noon, there was not a single bite, not a suspicion of one.

I wonder sometimes what size were those fish that so casually took my worms. Working out the breaking strain of the nylon line and allowing a generous margin, plus a following wind, a figure came which meant that, probably, each of them far exceeded the world record for bream. This is my consolation; it's easier to bear once you realise what you had been up against.

Memory is a distillation of the past and is not necessarily true, in that, whilst the flavour may be retained, the ingredients are disguised by time. Memory, playing tricks, concentrating many layers into one. Thus, it was that when, in order, to substantiate certain facts, I reread the Compleat Angler and saw that time, had indeed, mellowed some of the constituents over the period of nearly fifty years.

Isaak Walton gives a romantic view of his period, accurate for a privileged few, who had the means to enjoy leisure, as for example those retired or of independent means. He does so with honesty and without pretension and allows the milkmaid and the inn keeper to keep their dignity as befits their standing. He reflects the attitudes of the time and enthusiastically goes hunting with Venator and hounds, to kill otters including their young, because they eat fish. Furthermore, as a religious person he sees this act and them, as part of the intended order.

RF 1951

Now, my account seemed flowery and overblown after all the water which had passed under bridges in the intervening years. Youth had not then been soured by reality. Then, there were fewer boundaries, all was possible. Or to put it another way, it was pompous and pretentious. Ah well, such it is to be young!

But what lessons did I learn? How did they relate to my situation now? I recalled the smell of the mere, which was similar to the black ooze of the ponds but laced also with sweeter smells from the flowers around the lake. Smells have always been extremely evocative to me and in Brittany, on a beach near to Ploumanac, I had to run back to my car to pick up some snorkelling gear, which I had forgotten, probably my mask, which always seemed to hide away in a corner. When returning I tripped over a root or something and landed face down on a soil pathway.

Immediately, I could smell the rich dark brown odours of the earth on the banks in Big Bluebell wood. The smell was of mushrooms, wild garlic- or as we call them 'stinking onions'- campions and bluebell leaves but above all of 'pignuts'. I'm not a connoisseur of truffles but I know that pignuts have that same mustiness. We were told about them in the normal way by the 'older ones', the ones in the know; they knew everything, how to smoke elder pith (not recommended), how to make 'flop guns' (although my Grandfather was by far the best at this), how to suck eggs, the ways of lighting fires.

They had shown Bernard Foster, Howard Deane and me how to dig, down, into the dark brown earth, from leaves sprouting up from the surface that looked like carrot tops. Following a silver white slender stem, almost like a thread, down to approximately six or nine inches and there, if you were lucky, it was.

The shape was indeed that of a miniature white truffle and knobbly. With your fingers you could rub off the soil making the tips of your fingers brown and gritty. With a knife, finger nails - or even teeth - the outer skin could be taken off to reveal inside the white naked pignut. Raw, it tasted nutty with the aroma of deep dark damp woods. It could also be cooked when it then became a sort of potato with a chestnut flavouring.

Once I had started to recall such things from my childhood it was difficult to stop. One memory led to the next. The memories were pleasant with no overtones, no warnings. I just let my thoughts drift.

One day I went with my mates to collect wild water cress, which for some reason grows in abundance in Big Bluebell Wood. The wood had a fence completely surrounding it, but it was old and rotten and there was no difficulty in getting inside. There were three ponds, in two of which the water was almost black due to the leaves from the beeches, which each year fall in and rot. The effect was very threatening, and we knew that, if you fell in, there were also branches which could catch in your clothes and hold you down. On this particular Sunday we were also looking for waterhens' eggs and saw that there was, indeed, a nest in the middle of one of the black ponds. Being Sunday and having been to church, we were wearing suits, in fact mine was a new suit, a sort of tweedy brown with a light check pattern. There were three of us and no-one wanted to swim out to the nest, so we had to draw lots. Guess what – I lost! I had to undress until quite naked and then straddle a log or broken branch and paddle out rather than swim –oh! I did have on my underpants, so that I could stuff some eggs inside on the return journey.

Going out there was no problem and there were 15 eggs, so I tested them to see if they were 'addled' which, to us, meant they had chicks inside (this is done by seeing if they float; if they did, they were of no use). We always left enough to encourage the waterhens to lay more therefore I took ten. Coming back, with eggs in my pants and some in a handkerchief, was not so simple and half way the log rolled over and I went deep into the water. As I went down I discovered to my horror that there were some old branches under the surface; these scratched me, and it felt also that something like a bramble was holding me under. The feeling of terror was immediate. To be underneath that black water with what I knew to be smelly slimy, ooze at the bottom was the most horrendous thing you could imagine. Although it was only a split second before I surfaced, I felt like screaming, but of course I couldn't with the other two lads howling with laughter!

After I finally emerged, I found that there were six eggs saved; the rest were smeared all over me and I stank of fish and stagnant water (waterhens' eggs are very fishy). Fortunately, in the other part of the wood there was a stream of clearer water, where the cress grew, so I was able to strip and wash off, all the muck and egg yolks, wringing out my underpants after rinsing them.

By the time I was able to put my clothes back on, it had started to go dark, however, we shared the eggs, and, after picking some clumps of the cress, raced home. Unfortunately, whilst we could find our way in the dark, there were some parts where there was barbed wire fencing. In the gloom, and because I was running, I missed the gap and went straight into the barbed wire. My new best suit was torn, the triangular tear being about four inches long.

How I got away without this being discovered I do not know, but I was able to deliver the eggs and the wild watercress without any problem, and rush upstairs for a bath – hastily hanging up my suit out of the way. Over the next week, I secretly, invisibly mended the tear, using single threads from the inside of the sleeves and so successful was this repair that my parents never suspected the suit was damaged. At first, I kept my hand over the darn, so that it was hidden, but gradually I relaxed, and it became a source of youthful bravado to get away with it, and I would deliberately pose with the offending bit in full view. I told my mother only years after I married Sally and had two kids – I thought I was then fairly safe from retribution!

I realise, now, where my horror of sliding into the blackness in my dreams had originated. That moment in the pond could have easily been the end of my life. I also understood why I detested fog so much. So, my memories were giving me clues. They explained why my Dad had been so worried and not his normal self? Was *he* telling me this *now* in some way, guiding me? Ok, I knew why I felt guilty because I had stolen money and why certain things came up, but what to do next. Somethings were still hidden. How could I go forward? May be the lesson was that I had to read more to discover more clues Maybe it was not a dead end, but more of a cul-de-sac. Thinking about fishing, even, and the mishaps in the woods had made me realise why, now, I had certain thoughts. A childish mishap had been buried deep: my mother's accident even deeper. I *had* to do more.

Chapter 25

Thursday 20th March

The telephone rang and brought me back from my rather pointless reveries,

'It's me, Vera.'

'Hi Vera.'

'We must meet, I have just received back part of your father's notebook, deciphered.'

'What do you mean, deciphered?'

'Well, basically, they've cracked the code.'

'Wow, that's fantastic. Okay, I'm free anytime.'

'Right. Tomorrow … *your place or mine baby?*'

'Eh?'

'Only joking Rob, I thought you said that you watched the old movies? Ok, I'll come to your house. Would ten in the morning be okay?'

'Yes fine.'

'Shall I read? Or, since I've brought two copies, you can read, and I can follow on mine. Then I can stop to ask questions or, maybe, correct any errors if you spot them.'

'I'll read.'

'"When Alice told me that she was going to have a baby I was desperate. I'd no job having been dismissed from the dentist at the end of my apprenticeship. I was told by Vicky that Bert could possibly…".'

I broke off.

'What?' asked Vera.

'This is what I dreamt two days ago.'

'You have only just seen it. How could you dream about it?'

'I dreamt that I, *my dad*, that is, was talking to Cousin Bert and thanking him for getting me a job on the road navvying for the council and we talked about the baby that was coming and then my dad's dad, that's my Grandfather Foster, was telling my dad that he had got him an interview at ICI and, finally, I was my dad again in an interview with a Dr Freeth for the job in the new plant at Wallerscote.'

'But that's what is written down in his notes?'

'Well, I'm telling you, I dreamed about it.'

'Was there anything else? Did you dream anything more?'

'No, because then I woke up.'

'Ah, so there's more in these notes than you dreamt of. Carry on then from that note about his interview …'

'"In September 1935 when Rob was two years old, I went for an interview with Dr Freeth, the Research Director at ICI. He was personally recruiting university graduate chemists and men who had had secondary education. It seemed a good interview and he was particularly interested that I had been to grammar school, had worked with the vulcanisation of rubber and had used autoclaves. He also knew my father William Foster and that he had been a good runner, winning cups for the company team when it was still Brunner Mond, Obviously, I was considered to be suitable.

I started in December 1935 as a general labourer in the new pilot plant at Wallerscote. There was a small team of chemists led by Michael Perrin (he was a bit aloof) and other chemists like John Paton and Edmond Williams. There was little management, and the work was controlled by these chemists. They were trying to repeat and to improve the experiments by Eric Gibson and William Fawcett, who two years before, had made a small amount of waxy polythene. ICI had stopped the project after a while because the trials kept blowing up and it was considered to be too dangerous. There had been problems with Fawcett for disclosing at an open meeting the fact that ethylene could be polymerised, and he'd been sacked.

In December 1935, the equipment consisted of one 50ml autoclave, which had been the original reaction vessel and soon a new one of 750ml capacity, designed by the ICI engineer Dermot Manning. He was a nice chap and knew my dad.

This new reaction vessel was made from a more ductile type of steel which bent rather than shattered if there was an explosion. Because I had worked with the vulcanisation of rubber, I was soon involved in assisting with these experiments.

The chemists found out that there were leaks in the vessel due to the sealing valves not working over 300Atm, so Dermot redesigned special seals which deformed to the shape of the opening and fitted exactly under the higher pressures. We were now working with up to 2000Atm. The ethylene gas was supplied by BOC (British Oxygen Company) in large canisters which, when empty, were reused. It was found out that when they went back to BOC for refilling the valves were left open so letting in air. Then the chemists, with help from a professor at Oxford University, suggested the explosions were all to do with how much oxygen was in the mixture of gases. Perrin and Paton soon worked out that the ideal was 0.002% oxygen in the gas mixture and that over 2% it exploded.

Gradually we made progress and after 1936 when ICI finally applied for a patent for the process things became more urgent. First, they tried a 2litre reaction vessel then a 5litre one. On this latest one Dermot designed and added a blow-down valve which meant that polythene could be ejected without loss of pressure, thus it became a continuous process. There were still a few accidents and the engineers decided not to rebuild solid roofs in the reaction area but to make them of a lighter material, so the explosions went straight up and caused less damage to the plant.

The manufacturing improved although mixtures still exploded. I was made chargehand and then, in 1939, shift foreman. A large new reaction vessel of 50litres was installed to give 100 tonnes per year capacity. Soon afterwards a second one was installed.

The original use for the material was in undersea pipes and cables but then this use was stopped. We were called to a meeting and told that the new use was in wiring for special radios sets. After war broke out, we were also told that the product was vital for the war effort and not to talk about the process, and no interviews were given to the local newspapers. Three shifts were introduced and then these became two twelve-hour shifts as production expanded.

In addition to the production of the normal polythene pellets there were experiments with different catalysts resulting in mixtures of waxy polythene which could be used as a grease. They also produced different colours including a luminescent formulation which glowed in the dark. Because polythene is lighter than water it floated, and when I made Rob an aeroplane out of it, he loved it in his bath as it glowed when we turned the lights out.

In August 1940, production was again increased to double production, and as more staff were engaged, I was promoted to shift manager which also meant more pay. But this was the time when we started to have a series of unexplained problems. Plant would shut down for no reason, and relief valves, put in to prevent explosions when the reaction got out of control, were found blocked and so on.

I became very suspicious of one man, JD, who apparently had joined ICI in July 1940 and had worked as a lab assistant in the Alkali Division Research laboratory at Winnington. I then found out that he had requested a transfer to our small lab where the ethylene was checked for stray gases and the product was tested for consistency. Where he came from no one seemed to know. His accent was more southern than local.

In September I decided to keep a private log of the problems, times, dates etc".'

The rest of the diary was blank.

'Is that it?' I asked.

'That's all there is,' replied Vera.

'So, it goes up to September 1940 and then no more, when he decided to make a log.'

'Correct.'

'So, where's the log?'

'Ask me, I don't know,' Vera replied.

'I'm sorry if I sounded short. I feel cheated because I had thought we were going to hear a complete history. There's no mention of why he had a gun or where it came from - a spy gun at that, - nor anything to do with microdots. It's a complete dead end.'

'But you're forgetting those dates and funny dots which, comprise the log. This is just his record of the early history. Maybe he didn't want to write down what happened next, that is after September.'

'So, what now?'

'You notice that your Dad mentions his suspicions about JD, that could be the link. But who is JD and how do we find out?'

'That I don't know.'

'I think we should just wait and see whether anything comes back from those microdots.'

I racked my brain to see if I could throw any light on who might JD be. Eventually we might be able to obtain the details of the staff employed in the 1940s. but that would take time. My thoughts now seemed to be going around in circles as though the trail had ended or was complete, and there was nothing more to find out. There were other distractions, which came in the shape of a wedding and, less happily, the funerals of two members from the golf club. A week passed with no more news. Then Vera came to see me. She seemed different, not smiling, her cheeks were flushed.

She always looked attractive, with her blond hair now tending to platinum; her brown eyes twinkling as she made some quip. Her favourite dress colour appeared to be red but, today, I noticed that today she was wearing a more sombre brown. For some unknown reason I felt anxious, as I suspected she had some bad news.

'Are you all right?' I asked.

'Yes, I'm okay it's just that there have been developments. I believe that a lot of questions have been answered. But, *my* contact 'William' told me that it was out of his hands. The matter has been passed on and someone else has stepped in. Nobody would tell me any more than that, and I hope that it doesn't mean trouble for you.'

'My God, Vera what do you mean? Why should it?'

'Look I don't know, I've just been blocked, that's all, and I'm pretty cheesed off. I was told that someone would be coming to see you. but I can't even tell you who, or when.'

'Vera, you've done your best, and whatever happens, I promise to keep you informed. How's that?'

'Thanks, she said 'I just feel so bloody annoyed at being cut out of the loop.'

'Don't swear.' I said, my tongue firmly in my cheek. Vera got up to go and gave me a kiss.

'See you.' she said. Well! That was a first, I thought, and hoped that she would get mad more often.

I was as confused as Vera, but tried to stop myself from imagining the worst, a scenario where the police, or some ministry official, would appear to tell me off or read me the riot act. I remembered the last time that happened was when I forgot my flight bag on returning from Dublin by air. I was returning from a business trip and caught the last plane out of Dublin to Liverpool. It was February, there was no moon and the night was pitch black. The Liverpool airport was quite small in those days and the car park was unlit. Coming out of the bright fluorescent lights inside the airport terminal I was almost blind when I retrieved my car. I put my black flight bag on the ground at the back of the car, whilst loading up my suitcase into the boot. Then, because the bag was black, I didn't see it lying there and drove off.

It was during the time of 'The Troubles', and the bag was spotted by an airport official on a routine patrol. Security was alerted, and the bomb squad were called in. Fortunately, my business card was on a tag on the outside of the bag, with a link to my company, Yardale Plastics. They decided to check the contact number before they blew my bag up. Not that my MD was too pleased at being woken up at midnight to ask if he knew a Robert Foster.

A young whipper snapper from MI6 gave me a roasting the next day and suggested that, if I was getting too old to remember my luggage, maybe I shouldn't be travelling. Cross, I thought… *Where were you during the war, matey? I was part of the National Campaign helping to keep the health of the nation up by collecting rose hips with which to make the syrup with its high vitamin C content… So there!*

'I'm very sorry it won't happen again,' I replied meekly.

'Oh, and by the way, we noticed that there were cigarettes in the bag. Did you bring any more in your other luggage?'

Oh lord, I thought, now I'm going to be done for exceeding the allowance. But he had obtained his quota of satisfaction for today and just warned me like a schoolmistress wagging her finger… *You naughty boy, don't do it again!*

As Vera had suggested, might I be in line for another ticking off?' I didn't have long to wait. A few days after Vera told me the news, I received the telephone call.

Chapter 26

'Thank you for agreeing to see me. Do you know why I am here?'

I looked at this dapper man of about ninety dressed in blazer and flannels, who had arrived in a very expensive looking Rolls Royce saloon. We were sitting in the lounge and, thankfully, Sally was out for the day. The WI had a planned trip to some stately home or other, otherwise she would have been fussing about, worrying that she didn't have enough of this, or that she was ashamed because the carpet needed cleaning and so on.

He had piercing, light blue eyes which, even though they were set in a heavily lined face, almost seemed to twinkle.

'I'm not sure,' I replied honestly. What I did not mention was the dream I had had the night before, because it was only a dream wasn't it?

Vera had told me that she had been side-swiped and kept out of the loop but that somebody was going to contact me. What I suspected was that it was probably something to do with complications about that clip of polythene.

It wasn't, of course, the polythene itself, it was more likely the information contained in the microdots. The present manufacturers of polythene, Dupont, might have pointed out that this information had been obtained illegally, in effect stolen. Or had something arisen about the gun? His first words confirmed that I was correct.

'Mr Foster you *do* understand that what was on that polythene sample was stolen?'

'Yes, but I cannot believe that it had anything to do with my father. He didn't steal it.' I was ready to do battle.

Nevertheless, it was in your father's possessions, and it contained company information, in other words it was industrial espionage.'

'But this is crazy. I gave it to my friend—'

'Ms X is well known to us and it was through her actions that I am here today.'

'I see, it's Ms X is it now. How bizarre! By the way can I ask your name?'

'Certainly, which one would you like, Carruthers, Smith, Jones, I have plenty to offer. Course they're all fictitious.' I actually laughed, because it was clear now that he wasn't there to admonish me, he was enjoying himself. I relaxed.

'Okay, okay, I understand. You know, all I wished to know was whether it had anything to do with the polythene plant my dad worked in, and whether there was any connection with the gun. I presume you do know about that. Are you now going to tell me there could be trouble with … lawyers?'

I had had problems with lawyers all my working life. They tried to make money out of simple errors and accidental misuse of patents.

I remembered one case where a trade mark of ours was being contested by a large national company on the grounds that there could be confusion with their own. The whole thing was being blown up out of all proportion by lawyers until I had lunch with their MD. We agreed it would cost both companies totally unnecessary lawyers' fees, and we should just forget the dispute. There never was any confusion of products.

'Don't worry about lawyers,' he replied smiling. 'Because these microdots originated during the early years of World War II, when Ms X's report went to MI6, it was passed on to the Archived Operations Section IV and, out of courtesy, eventually, to me.

Whilst I am now retired, during my active service, I was personally involved in what happened at the Wallerscote plant.

The diary added to the information which we had and, as it were, completed the circle. I requested permission to discuss this matter with you personally. This was accepted.'

'Okay Mr Carruthers…I rather like the sound of that you know. Well what news have you got?'

'Now that we have broken the ice as it were, please call me David and may I call you Robert, or would you prefer your nickname, Rob?' I shook my head in wonder, the whole interview was becoming truly bizarre. And how the hell did he know my nickname?

'Yes, Dave that will be great, although I may still remember you as Mr Carruthers. Can we also call Ms X, Vera?'

'Of course. Then be patient and I will tell you the whole story.

'Would you like coffee or tea?' floated in round the door.' My God, she was back, the WI trip must have been called off.

'Coffee for both of us would be splendid, Sally.' Dave shouted back.

'How in God's name do you know *her* name?' I gasped, flabbergasted. Dave tapped his nose,

'We know a lot about you Rob.'

The coffees came,

'Nice car,' Sally said as she exited, 'I hope the farmer doesn't bring his cows down, they can make a hell of a mess if they decide to crap on it.' It was my turn to grin as I saw the look of horror on his face.

'She's only winding you up, you probably parked where she normally does. Please do carry on.'

'As a counter espionage officer during the war, in the August of 1940, I was briefed to investigate problems, which were suspected to be acts of sabotage at the Wallerscote Polythene Plant. As you know, I am sure, its product was essential to the development of radar. Our fighter planes were shooting down the German bombers at night, because we could track them with radar. And, they didn't know how. We even put out the story that it was because the pilots ate a lot of carrots. It was a complete fabrication, of course, but it worked.

I was privileged to know and work with your father, Earnest Foster, or Ernie, who was a shift foreman at the time.'

'You worked with my father?' My jaw must have dropped to the floor.

'Yes, for several months. I had had passed on to me a timetable showing dates and possible correlation to the problems in the plant. You know that several men were killed in explosions?'

'Yes.'

'The incidents were believed to have started after the crash of a Dornier at Winsford—'

'I remember that,' I exclaimed. 'There was a photograph taken at the time and printed in the Northwich Gazette – I mean Guardian,' I said correcting myself. 'In fact, I think the whole family remembered it because one of my uncles was in the photograph.'

'That I didn't know, but to continue. The pilot was badly injured, captured and interned but later died. Although the pilot would not confirm our suspicion, we believe that there had been another occupant in the aeroplane, a passenger who had bailed out. He was never captured, at least not at the time.

As I said, the polythene plastic was vital to the war effort, particularly for high voltage systems such as radar. Because it was in such great demand production was doubled. New staff were taken on. It was then that we believe the spy called Zeissmann was taken on as a laboratory technician—'

'So Vera's information was right! I interrupted.

'Yes, her information was perfectly correct. His alias was John Charles Dunn. He'd studied for a degree at Oxford, his English was perfect, and there was no reason to suspect him at the time—'

'Wrong!'

'How do you mean?'

My Dad had his suspicions very soon after Dunn came into the lab.' I recalled my father's notes about JD, and whilst Vera hadn't cracked the code completely, it all fitted. 'I bet it's all there in my father's diary. He made notes which clearly linked the problems, that is the explosions and breakdowns, to shifts and dates.'

'Well, that doesn't surprise me because of what happened. My cover was that I was employed as Safety Officer and could therefore roam about more freely.'

On the 23rd January 1941 on the evening shift that your father happened to be on, I heard a scuffle and shouts. I ran in to the engineering section and saw Dunn on the floor. Your father was standing over him holding a heavy wrench and shouting,

'You bloody Nazi!'

Neither had noticed me but, as I ran towards them, Dunn suddenly pulled out a gun and was about to shoot your father, so I shot him, one to the head and one to the heart. He was killed outright.

Your father was in shock, naturally, so I grabbed him and told him that I was a Secret Service officer and the man, I had shot, was a German spy. His name wasn't Dunn, it was Zeissmann. Then I said that he was to do exactly as I told him. I said to take the saboteur's gun and throw it into the river and that I would clean things up before the others came to investigate. He did as I asked, or, as things now appear, not completely. For some reason he kept the gun.

After your dad had knocked Zeissmann down, he must have picked up that production sample, the one with microdots embedded in it, knowing that Dunn should not have had it. Maybe

Zeissmann had dropped it or it fell out of his pocket. I suspect that after I had shot and killed Zeissmann, in the excitement your dad forgot all about it, until sometime later when he found that it contained those microdots. Why he then kept quiet about the microdots I don't know, and I knew nothing about their existence until you passed them on.

It is now obvious that Zeissmann was trying to get the details of the plant back to his masters, somehow…probably through Ireland. I had believed that Zeissmann's only object was to sabotage the plant. It was more, much more. That's why I said before that the information you passed on to us allowed us to complete the circle. Had he succeeded who knows what effect it would have had.'

'But that wasn't the whole story, was it?' I said.

'No. After your dad left, I made it look like an accident to hide the bullet wounds, as though some heavy gear had fallen onto Dunn, and covered him up. As Safety Officer it was fairly easy to disguise what had happened, even the shots were explained later as falling machinery.

Your dad was angry when he came back and said,

'I knew there was something queer about that bugger. It was too much of a coincidence that most of the explosions occurred when he was on the shift. And remember, some of my workmates were killed. I did a chart…'

'I told him to go home and forget about it, but to come in as normal the following day and we would talk privately. I also contacted my section who immediately came and removed the body to avoid any problems with the local police.

The next day, as arranged, your father came to see me. He looked pale and I told him it was only natural, bearing in mind what had happened, but that he must swear never tell anyone. He said, of course, he was shaken but he was getting over that, and it was good to know that that bastard had been stopped. It was Alice, his wife. He was very worried about her.

He explained what had happened last year when she fell, and then how, over the months, she had become worse. She was now bedridden and couldn't even look after her boy.

'That was you, of course,' Carruthers said, and I nodded.

Your dad went on to explain that the doctors had warned him that she was dying, and that there was nothing they could do. At this point your dad could hardly hold back his tears. Apparently, she had had a bad turn the night before and he didn't know what to do. I told him that if I could, I would help, and it so happened that I did have an idea.

One of my contacts was a friend of a brilliant young orthopaedic surgeon, a Mr Watson Jones, who specialised in problems of this nature, lecturing and operating on "fractions" as they were called at the time. Apparently he had published several articles, including a book, on "Fractures and Joint Injuries". He was very involved with the treatment of injured airmen, pilots, and the like, particularly during and after the Battle of Britain. Obviously, he, like other surgeons, was under tremendous pressure, but he managed to find time to rearrange his schedule. The rest is, as you know, history. Your mother was transferred immediately to Liverpool General Infirmary and was seen by him and operated on two days later.

Are you all right, Robert?' he said addressing me.

'Yes,' I sniffed, welling up. 'You have answered all my questions and more. My mother, who's still alive and kicking, told my dad that, when Watson Jones examined her, he just said, "I can cure you", and he did. We didn't understand exactly how he treated her, but she told us that it involved traction.

I didn't know it at the time but my mother, because of her fall, had suffered a vertebral compression fracture. It is now known to occur twice as often as hip fractures, but in these early days the science and treatment was in its infancy, almost non-existent. If a spinal fracture was left untreated, the vertebra could heal in the 'broken' position leading to a forward curvature. The misaligned spine then compressed the internal organs leading to serious health problems, which is exactly what happened to my mother. Reading, later, about Sir Reginald Watson-Jones, as he became, I now realize that your 'young orthopaedic surgeon friend' was, and still is, regarded as one of the greatest surgeons in his field and his achievements are legendary. We cannot thank you enough for helping my mother and father.'

I then explained to Carruthers - Dave still seemed disrespectful - about my own accident and the injury to my head, and how I had been having these odd flashbacks, but I didn't know why they seemed to point to my mother and father. I still don't know, but you have explained how he acted, and I suppose that he kept that Luger and the piece of polythene on the spur of the moment.

'Well, he was, of course, sworn not to tell a soul, no one *not even your mother*. He let her believe that Mr Watson's presence in Liverpool, just at the right time, was a happy coincidence, a miracle. There was no question of any mention, officially. We never admitted that there were spies operating in England, you see: it would have been bad for morale.

That little diary, by the way, conceals a list of what happened during those shifts which he suspected were being sabotaged. It mentioned the valves, which should have been open but were closed, and vice versa. He didn't tell anyone, but he did leave the clues in his diary. He was a clever man, your father, I believe that he wanted *you* to know the truth.'

As Carruthers came to the end of his story he added.

'One thing puzzled me at the time and I asked him how he became aware that this man was going to attack him. He said that he was standing with his back to Zeissmann, or Dunn, as he knew him at the time, attending to one of the valves that was sticking, when he heard a voice shout,

"*Behind you …Dad!*" But he must have been mistaken, mustn't he?'

After shaking hands with me and thanking Sally for the coffee, he left. Later that afternoon Vera rang. She sounded happier and said that she was coming to see me that evening, if that was all right. I said there was no problem and told her that I had had a certain visitor. She said she knew. Sally was used to Vera visiting, and rustled up two teas and a coffee without even asking. There were even chocolate-chip biscuits thrown in. After Sally had finished her tea and, knowing that she had done her duty, she excused herself and went out to a WI meeting; maybe it was instead of the trip, I thought.

'I know most of the story about your dad and I'm impressed,' she said. 'So, who goes first?'

I'll start off,' I said and recounted what Mr "Carruthers" had told me as to what had happened that night at the plant. She listened in silence until I had finished. Then she asked,

'But who warned your Dad?'

'I did,' I replied. I told her that the night before I had met Carruthers, I had had the perfect dream, in which my Dad and I sat together fishing on Marbury Mere until the sun went quietly down. But that then, after we packed up and cycled home, my dream took me to the polythene plant.

I recognised the characteristic smell of hot polythene and was aware of the hum coming from the control valves and pumps thumping away.

It was dark except for low level essential lighting. Then I saw my Dad who, somehow, I knew, was checking pressures in a reaction vessel because one of the valves was tending to stick. To my horror I saw a tall shadow creeping up behind him with a heavy iron bar in his hand. I realised immediately who it was. It was Zeissmann the spy, alias Dunn.

I felt the pressure in my head that I had had in those other experiences, but now no dizziness. I knew what was going to happen. At that moment I focussed on the fact that my Dad was in danger. There was only one thing to do.

'Behind you Dad.' I shouted. The rest is as Mr Carruthers, or Dave, told me.

'So, you believe that this is what all those dreams were about, then,' said Vera. 'That *somehow* you were able warn your dad. I really cannot believe it, you know. But neither can I explain how it could have happened any other way. It was what Carruthers told you, that your Dad said to him at the time. Why would he lie?' she shook her head.

'I didn't believe it myself but there it is. My dad wasn't killed. He had some instinct to keep the gun and the polythene with the data on it. Without those, and the clues, which he deliberately left, I would never have known the truth. And what if, as my *black dreams* showed me, he had been killed, and Zeissmann had got the information back to Germany. What then?'

'Ah, then, now it's my turn. Let me tell you my story,' said Vera, eyes once more flashing in triumph. 'I can dot the 'I's and cross the 'T's. I'll start at the beginning.

In 1938 MI5, that is the British security service, were aware that Zeissmann had disappeared, but the Germans had another version. He was active in many areas including Australia and Canada, where he was unchallenged, and could move about unnoticed, invisible. As a degree chemist he was in great demand and was able to funnel information back to Germany fairly easily about any interesting developments.

In 1939, the chemists at I.G. Farben were wondering whether there was anything in the rumours, which were surfacing, about the new plastic, polyethylene. They had the patent, they had a sample, but it seemed, according to their latest information, that the process was too dangerous and unpredictable to be of much use. Typically, German, however, they wanted to check it out and were able to interest the Abwehr.

In early 1940 Zeissmann was secretly recalled to Germany and given a thorough briefing. His task was to determine whether ICI had managed to develop a successful process for the manufacture of polyethylene and, if so, to obtain data and plans of the equipment. They also were intrigued as to what were its main uses.

The first problem they had was that they did not know where the plant might be. Because they had the information about all the known divisions and what they made, they were able to eliminate all, except for ICI Winnington which was where the first experiments had been made. They could not be sure if it was there but that is where they decided to send Zeissmann.

In June 1940 they sent a lone Dornier bomber to drop him by parachute onto the Peak District near to Macclesfield. Unfortunately, the plane was picked up by radar and shot down near to Winsford. Zeissmann narrowly escaped capture and laid low until the bombing raids on London diverted attention elsewhere. With his perfect accent and knowledge, he applied for a job in the labs at Winnington. Very quickly he established his skills and, when he requested a transfer to the new polythene plant, it was granted immediately.

Getting to know the process was easy and the chemists were only too eager to discuss the problems. He even made some useful improvements, but, when in October he saw how successful they were, he started to sabotage parts in the hope of slowing the development down. He finally made his plans and, with the microdots safely in his possession, determined to cause a large explosion and then, in the furore, disappear, getting back to Germany through Ireland. That's it; he would have made it except for your Dad.'

'And who knows, I suppose it *is* possible that my mother, by some miracle, might have been cured anyway,' I said, but didn't believe it.

Vera and I hugged. We were both crying. Then she returned to her normal feisty self.

Chapter 27

And that was the end of it as far as I was concerned, but it wasn't. A week later Vera telephoned me,

'Rob, I think you should prepare yourself for a big shock.'

'No more shocks, *please*. It's all over and done with now. We know what happened, enough is enough.'

'You're right we know what happened but what about Zeissmann?'

'Vera, he died in 1941. I don't know any more about him, not even where he was buried ... and I didn't ask. It would have been an unknown grave, or possibly buried at sea. No-one has said anything about it.'

'You are correct, but something has arisen ... he left a daughter.'

'A daughter?'

'Yes, her name is Mary Jane, Mary Jane Dunn.'

'Isn't that an English name. '

'Yes, she was born and lives in Smithfield. But, will you just hold all your questions until I see you – don't spoil my story. Okay if I pop round?'

'Yes, of course ... what *now?*'

'I'll be round in half-an-hour ... tell Sally to put the kettle on.'

When I told Sally, she said that *this time* she wanted to hear the story from the organ grinder ...

So *now* I'm the monkey, I thought.

'Mary Jane Dunn was born in 1937, in Smithfield,' said Vera, reading from her notes.

'*Where*? Smithfield? Isn't that a market in London?'

'Yes, it is, but this is *not* Smithfield, England, it's Smithfield, *Australia*.'

'Jumpin' Jehosphat', said Sally excitedly. I know Smithfield, Australia… that's near to Cairns… It's not too far from where we farmed. … So … she's Australian!'

'Correct. When the German authorities got hold of Zeissmann's gun and heard the details of his death, they wanted to compile a dossier on his life. After all, what he did was to spy for Germany, and he died in the course of his activities. We've concentrated on one side of the coin – your Dad's side. And that has been fully explained, but there is the other side.

Anyway, you know nowadays that there are all sorts of ways of tracking ancestors, particularly when you have something like the German State wanting to find out the information and picking up the bill. They discovered that there was a girl, a waitress in Sydney in 1936, a Rosemary Beckett, who had a liaison with Zeissmann – although he wasn't called Zeissmann then, of course; his alias was Dunn, John Charles Dunn. The result was that Rosemary became pregnant'

'JC! Jesus Christ, you know that's a damned good old English name for a German spy. 'interjected Sally– Sorry about that … couldn't resist.' Vera gave her that look, which previously had been reserved for me.

'… And don't swear,' I said sternly to Sally, only to have that freezing look redirected. Vera knew that I was taking the Mickey.

'When you've finished, is it okay to continue?' Vera said. Sally and I kept mum.

'Dunn had impeccable credentials, which could be traced back to Cambridge, if anyone had bothered to check, and why should they in those pre-war days? Anyway, there was no marriage; it seems to have been a short-lived affair, and the girl's parents were so ashamed that they packed her off to a cousin, Dick and his wife, Dulcie Beckett, who farmed near to Cairns, which is where the child, a girl was born. The birth certificate confirms the mother as Rosemary Beckett and the father as John Dunn, presumably because Mary did not know about Dunn's middle name

Christened as Mary Jane Dunn, she turned out to be a clever girl and obtained a 1st Class Honours BSc from Brisbane University in 1958, where she met and married, in 1968, one Wilhelm Kent – his parents had interestingly changed their surname from Kanz to Kent when they emigrated from Austria in 1946. The Kents have a successful vineyard in Nappa Valley. Mary Jane Dunn became the Scientific Officer for her husband's parents' vineyard 'Crowning Glory' and several others. Mary and Willy have four children who all work in the wine trade. Mary Jane's mother died in 1985.

'Howma' doin?' We had listened spellbound, even Sally was dumbstruck.

'Oh, and here's the punchline, Mary Jane wants to meet you, if you are agreeable.'

'But how did she get to know my name? And what has she been told? I'm not sure that I'm ready for this'

'I think she has been given the basics i.e. that her dad was an agent working for the Third Reich in the German Intelligence Service and died in the course of his duties. In other words, in German eyes, he's a hero. The man with whom Dunn had worked in Cheshire died in 1968, but they informed her that his son was alive and lived now in Yorkshire.'

I had been trying to get my head around *my* problems and to discover what now appeared to be the definitive truth about my father and my mother's miraculous cure. Now there was another dimension, a path leading to another country and continent.

The spy, whom my Dad had called "a Bloody Nazi" and so on, and who was involved in his killing, had a fifty-eight-year-old daughter, with four children. Apart from Carruthers, I was, through my father, the closest remaining link to her father's death. I wondered how she would feel about that. No matter what, she was his daughter. If Dunn, or Zeissmann, was forced to abandon her mother because he was under orders then it would make the abandonment more understandable and acceptable. I could understand her wish to follow it up; to get to the bottom of what happened. She was only doing what I'd been doing. How could I refuse to meet her?

We suggested a date for Mary Jane to come across to Yorkshire, if that was convenient, and, when it was confirmed, booked her into the Devonshire at Bolton Abbey, a favourite of mine, particularly because it was where our daughter Jackie had her wedding reception.

It was felt better that, initially, I would meet Mary Jane alone, to break the ice. So, it was arranged that I would pick her up from Manchester airport and take her to the Devonshire. Fortunately, I had been signed off and allowed to start driving again. My Volvo was in pristine condition, all the bumps and gouges had been removed, and it had been resprayed in a lighter, metallic blue colour, much better than the original.

Mary Jane was a stocky woman with the palest of blond hair, almost white. She looked younger than fifty-eight, partly because of her deeply tanned but unlined skin. Her eyes were light blue, clearly, I thought because of her father's genetic makeup. Her voice was soft and her "G—day, nice to meet you" was not too accented. I liked her immediately.

She was understandably tired from the journey, and we just talked about small things on the way to the hotel. She had been to England before but not Yorkshire, and the stone walls and small size of the fields amazed her, even the sheep were small, she said. I told her that they were used to living high up on the moors sometimes in wet and cold conditions. She immediately said that she would like to see the moors and, in particular, The Bronte country round Haworth.

Arriving at the Devonshire I said that she should sleep and suggested that we could meet the next day for lunch. I made sure that she had our home telephone number in case she had any problems - it was no use giving her a mobile number because there was no signal half the time in Gardale.

After lunch we had a drink in a quiet corner of the lounge. In fact, before I had finished *my* story we'd had several refills. Then we arranged to have an evening meal together with Sally and, because she was boiling over with curiosity, Vera, who on this occasion behaved herself.

Now that my side of the story had been told, it was naturally Sally who told Anne about *her* father's death in the outback and the sisters' migration to Canada and how we had met. Obviously, certain details were glossed over, and I was conscious that Vera was listening to every word, analysing, no doubt to quiz me later.

Mary Jane was satisfied now to have the inside story and felt that she could relate the tale to her children. She had four, two boys and two girls all of whom were employed in the wine trade. Sally had indicated that she would like to pay a visit to where her mum and dad had had their ranch even though they were both dead and only cousins left out there. Though we didn't mention it the idea was firmed up when Mary Jane invited us - and Vera - to stay with them.

Vera and I were recapping the events of the last year and looking forward to the millennium. I had promised to do some leg-work for her researches, which was an excuse on my part to keep seeing her.

We had indeed been out to Australia in what was their autumn, accepting Mary Jane's kind offer, and met the family and seen the local sights. Their hospitality was outstanding to what were strangers, including one of whose father had been involved in the death of their grandfather. There was no love for the Nazis, however, particularly from Mary Jane's father and mother in law. They'd had their own experiences in Austria.

We went on to Cairns and met Sally's relatives where, once again, we were received royally. Id let slip about Vera's intelligence work, much to her dismay, and they wanted to know if she'd met Sean Connery.

Back in England we settled back down into our normal routine and after a while, I realised that we had come to the end of the intense detective work; the sort of activity which had made Vera's eyes shine. I'd run out of ideas and was starting to vegetate. Not so Vera. One week later we were in the library.

'Now then, what about that uncle Ron of yours and that Dornier. Why was he there? Was he a spy too?!'

Epilogue

2030

I'd decided to write down the story of my strange hallucinations, if that is what they were, but realise that there's nothing about Jackie and Pam growing up, their first steps, their first words, their crises, and development through childhood to adulthood. Nothing about my brother, Tom, and his family,

The account is how my mind was directed back to those early childhood days *before* my mother's accident, and then my guilt, because I was the cause of it. I understand, now, that the purpose was to follow my Dad's clues, to save my mother's life by saving his. I was so happy to discover what my father did for my mother, whom he loved to bits and likewise.

Neither is it written in this account, what Vera and I discovered after spending many happy months tracing the story behind the Dornier crash and Uncle Ron's involvement; that's another story.

We also traced Vera's ancestors back to the 1700s. Then, we started on Sally's history, which quickly became a who-done-it, embedded with crime and transportation. Sally thought it was a hoot to discover that her Great, Great, Great, Grandfather had four wives, sired forty children, and had robbed a bank.

Hopefully, someone will pick up these notes and create their own story for those who follow us.

My mother passed away in 2006, the day after her 96th birthday, still feisty to the end. Richard passed away in 2004, another old golf partner gone. Many relatives and friends quietly departed leaving their own pools of grief but also the happiness from their lives and the promise from the youngsters. I was devastated when Vera died suddenly in 2010; mortality was catching up with us all.

I could never understand how the miracle, which cured my Mum had occurred, and above all was grateful for the work of that brilliant surgeon who carried out the operation and countless others. He gave her a life. A life to run over the fields; a life to play with her children and grandchildren; a life to give her love to others, anyone who needed it. A full and rewarding life.

I've had a good innings and didn't think it would be long before one or other of my ailments caught up with me. The stroke made it harder to finish the story, because it became extremely difficult to think of the correct words. Also, whether it was the stroke or the arthritis, I started keying the wrong letters onto the computer. As Morecombe said, "they are the right notes, just in the wrong order". Any way that's it. It's finished now.

Somehow or other, they let me stay at home - maybe it was Sally's very persuasive tongue. In any case, I didn't want to be regularly re-hydrated, ventilated or resuscitated. I told Sally that I had always loved her, and she called me a soppy old codger, so that was all right.

Each day, the sheep in the field opposite, seen through the front window, appear to get further and further away. The sky seems darker.

I am not frightened any longer about those black visions, I don't think there will be any …

The hills have all disappeared and a level plain stretches out before me. There is no darkness.

I am not worried by this place, all that I had to do I have done, and I can now just stride out. There are no aching limbs nor painful joints, no breathlessness. No need to rush. I am going north but the sun is ahead, that is the way of things.

I perceive, peripherally, that there are others converging, walking with me; more and more join the path. I recognise some; there's Dopey Dicky from school, on the other side there's Mike McGiloway from Canada, he waves; Pamela and Joan who I played tennis with at Winnington. Vera and Richard went some years ago but more ... and yet more come, until the land is filled with ramblers. Then I see the numerous golfing friends, John and Jack, Albert and Frank. Those closest turn and smile.

Ahead, I see the house, our old house, standing proudly above the plain. It's surrounded by a low white fence that I don't remember but at the gate I see a small crowd of people waiting.

My mother, my father, Granny Walker, and Grandpa Walker who made me flop-guns; Granny Foster, and Grandad Foster, who taught me how to play chess; aunts and uncles.

They are all there just waiting patiently for me to arrive, arms open…

****

Acknowledgements

The object of this story is twofold. Firstly, to put down in writing a flavour of things, which happened many years ago; mere vignettes from earlier days. It is a work of fiction and where desirable names, places, events, and characters have been changed. Some places are real; some of the incidents are based on fact, others have been changed to suit the story.

Secondly, and mainly, I wanted to record the gratitude of our whole family, my mother in particular, to Sir Reginald Watson-Jones, who died in 1972, and surgeons like him, for their incredible achievements.

What he did for my mother was not fiction, it was a true miracle and without his timely intervention, this story could not have been written.

Sir Reginald Watson-Jones Kt, MRCS, FRCS, BSc, MCH Orth, MB ChB, LRCP, Hon FACS, Hon FRACS, Hon FRCS Ed, Hon FRCS Canada, KSTJ, was born Reginald Jones on the 4th of March 1902, the youngest child of Edward Henry Jones, a senior officer working for Dr Barnado's Homes, and his wife Alice, née Watson. His father worked first at Brighton and then at Liverpool, where the younger Jones received his schooling.

After contracting typhoid in his youth, the younger Jones decided on a career in medicine and set his heart on orthopaedic surgery after he underwent an operation to remove a haemangioma. He joined the Medical School of Liverpool University, graduating with a first-class Bachelor of Science degree in 1922, his Bachelor of Medicine and Surgery degrees two years later, and a Masters of Orthopaedic Surgery in 1926. He would be remembered as one of the school's "most brilliant then and since", winning numerous prizes. He was named Mitchell Banks Medallist (1920), George Holt Medallist (1921) and Robert Gee Prizeman (1923). In 1921, he received the Senior Lyon Jones Scholarship and two years later took the George Holt Fellowship in Physiology, before receiving the Samuel's Research Scholarship in Surgery in 1926. In 1923 he became a demonstrator in Anatomy and Physiology and received the Conjoint Diploma at Liverpool in 1924.

Jones became a surgeon at Liverpool Royal Infirmary and Great Ormond Street Hospital after qualifying in medicine. While at Liverpool he blossomed under the guidance of the eminent surgeon Robert Jones (of no relation), who recommended him to be appointed honorary assistant surgeon at the Infirmary in 1926. In 1927 he was appointed a fellow of the Royal College of Surgeons.

Jones was appointed a surgeon at the Country Orthopaedic Hospital at Gobowen and took up an honorary position at North Wales Sanatorium. He began publishing articles in the Journal of Bone and Joint surgery in the early 1930s and produced an average of three a year from then on. His contributions earned him recognition and he began teaching a popular course on fractions at Liverpool University in 1936, which prompted him to work on a textbook; Fractures and Joint Injuries, which appeared in 1940, was reprinted and translated many times and called a "masterpiece". Its clear and accessible language meant that it became a valued guidebook to field surgeons in World War II. In 1937 Jones changed his surname to Watson-Jones, using his mother's maiden name, to distinguish himself from the many other people called Jones at the hospital, including his mentor Robert Jones.

During the early years of World War II, Watson-Jones remained a civilian consultant to the Royal Air Force. He set up ten units of 100–150 beds each across the United Kingdom to house recovering pilots; his emphasis on rehabilitation meant that 77% were able to return to active service. In 1942, he established the Department of Orthopaedics and Accidents at the London Hospital and in 1945 he was knighted for his service to the war efforts. Three years later, he was instrumental in establishing the British volume of the *Journal of Bone and Joint Surgery* (BJBJS) and became its editor (serving until his death). He spoke out against the establishment of the National Health Service, writing in 1948 that private practice was an essential component of medical progress. Meanwhile, he was a member of the Royal College of Surgeon's Council between 1943 and 1959; he was appointed the College's Hunterian Professor in 1945 and Sims Commonwealth Travelling Professor in 1950, before serving as Vice-President in 1953–54; he delivered the Hunterian Oration in 1959. He was also Orthopaedic Surgeon to George VI from 1946 to 1952 and Extra Orthopaedic Surgeon to Elizabeth II from 1952 to his death, as well as President of the Orthopaedic Section of the Royal Society of Medicine in 1956, and of the British Orthopaedic Association in 1952–53. Watson-Jones's surgical work was characterised by meticulous attention to detail and precision, and he expected no different from his students, while he kept unusually detailed and orderly notes on all his consultations. His work, especially during the war, but before it too, brought new ways of treating fracture into mainstream medical practice, and his publications and work with the BJBJS meant that they were available for surgeons across the world to use.

  Watson-Jones married twice: firstly in 1930 to Muriel Emily, daughter of Charles William Cook, who died in 1970, and secondly, a year later, to Muriel Wallace Robertson, a nurse; he adopted two children (a son and a daughter) with his first wife. He died 9th August 1972. His obituaries call him a "warm and attractive man ... a very great 'doctor' and one of the outstanding orthopaedic surgeons of his generation". Another study of his life states that, along with his mentor Robert Jones, he "laid the foundation for a strong history of British orthopaedics".

Bibliography]

A selection of Watson-Jones's publications is listed below

- *Fractures and Joint Injuries*, 1st edition (1940) and 5th edition (1969)
- *Pye's Surgical Handicraft* (1938) and 15th edition (1953)
- *Medicine and Surgery for the Attorney*, British edition

References

1. Osmond-Clarke, H., "Sir Reginald Watson-Jones, M.Ch.Orth., F.R.C.S., F.R.C.S.Ed., F.R.C.S.C., F.R.A.C.S., F.A.C.S.", *Annals of the Royal College of Surgeons of England*, vol. 51, issue 4 (October 1972), p. 265–266
2. Hagy, Mark, "'Keeping up with the Joneses' – the story of Sir Robert Jones and Sir Reginald Watson-Jones", *Iowa Orthopedic Journal*, vol. 24 (2004), pp. 133–137
3. "Sir Reginald Watson-Jones", *Times* (London), 11 August 1972, p. 14
4. "Watson-Jones, Sir Reginald", *Who Was Who* (online edition), Oxford University Press, April 2014. Retrieved 29 September 2016.

5. Bentley, George, "Jones, Sir Reginald Watson- (1902–1972)", *Oxford Dictionary of National Biography*, Oxford University Press, 2004
6. *The London Gazette*, 31 August 1937 (issue 34431), p. 5542

Notes:

These were written by Sir Reginald Watson-Jones, by hand - now acting as physiotherapist - listing the exercises my mother was to carry out, daily, during her rehabilitation.

1. Crook Lying Abdominal Contractions
2. Lying a Legs crossed gluteal contractions
3. Lying Pressing Knees against bed (Quadriceps Contractions)
4. Forward Lying Alternate leg lifting with straight Knee.
5. Crook Lying Pelvic Tilting, that is pressing lower part of back against bed & lifting buttock off bed pressing Knees together
6. Lying alternate leg shortening
7. Crook Lying Breathe in expanding ribs (Breathe in through nose mouth closed) Breathe out through mouth
8. Sitting Elbows circling
9. Combine 1, 2, & 3
10. Forward Lying Head and shoulders raise off bed (Grasp hands behind)
11. Standing between 2 chairs. Heels raised and lower, R foot forwards Heels raise lower Repeat with L foot
12. Walking
13. Crook lying. Pull in Abdominal muscles Raise head off bed pulling in chin
14. Crook lying. Raise back off bed, slowly lower pulling in Abdominal muscles.

15. Crook Lying R hand to L knee, L hand to R knee, Both to both knees
16. Crook lying R knee touch nose, L knee touch nose, Both knees touch nose
17. Crook lying touch R ankle. Up straight. Bending touch L ankle. Up straight.